Where No One Follows

By Peggy Godson Mueller

ISBN: 978-1-959788-04-1

CHAPTER ONE

Whenever we speak of the past in our small town of Burnt Willow, we refer to events in terms of "before it happened" and "after it was over." No deliberate mention is made of one particular year – only an occasional slip-up to which the guilty party flinches and abruptly stops talking, realizing he'd spoken the unspeakable, afraid he may have cracked open Pandora's box.

I have tried to piece together that part of my early history from those brief slips of the tongue I've overheard. As distasteful as it is for most to conjure up thoughts of "it", I find myself trying to recall as much as I can. However, my memory is a bit hazy, and it is difficult to discern between the truth and my active imagination. One might call my story a work of fiction, but to me it's painfully real. I liken it to that time in the morning when your eyes slowly open after a particularly vivid dream. You lie in your half-slumber for a moment, unable to move, only to have most memories of the dream flee instantly upon your first stretch.

I stretched. Or perhaps I purposely jarred myself awake from the confusing nightmare when it was over, a safe distance away, so memories of it wouldn't linger. I am now fully awake and have developed much curiosity and strength enough to confront the pain of my seventh year on this planet – the year twelve of us became phantoms, leaving behind our content lives and most of our worldly belongings, disappearing into the whispered legends of Burnt Willow's history.

And so, I begin my tale with Knock.

When I saw Knock for the fourth time in my young life, I knew he was there for a special purpose. He had helped me through difficult times, and I knew in my heart he would remain nearby until I took my last breath. Though we'd never exchanged many words, his eyes – robin's egg blue, calming, reassuring – spoke to me in streams of pure contentment as he peered out from under eyebrows much too dark for his fair complexion.

In my haste to tell Paw that Knock was waiting out back, I violated rules number one and two – don't interrupt Paw if he's speaking with a customer and never run in the garage.

"Lulu, you know you're not supposed to be out here. You could get yourself hurt. Now go and play outside," he said, shooshing me away with his grease-blackened hand.

Paw continued explaining the function of a fan belt to a disinterested-looking gentleman as I turned to leave. I politely walked out of Paw's sight and then took off, rocket speed, to tell Knock he would need to wait a while longer and to offer him a root beer. He was no longer standing behind the garage next to the metal gasoline drums, so I ran around to the side gravel parking lot and flew the rest of the garage's perimeter before giving up my search for him. Disappointment quickly turned into an assurance that I would see him again soon. My intuition was a special gift, my mother told me, so I knew I was right.

Paw came into the small waiting area where I had plopped myself down on the grimy rug, listening to the tinny whine of country music coming from the radio which stayed propped on a stack of telephone books in the corner. I took a large gulp of cold Coke, patted my belly and belched as Paw stood in front of me. I grinned. Paw did not.

"'Scuse me."

"What was so all-fired important a second ago?" he grumbled. I couldn't tell if he was angry or grimacing because of the sweat rolling into his eyes. "Well?" he asked, wiping his brow with the tail of his shirt.

"Knock was here. I thought he needed to ask you something."

With a slow shake of his head he replied, "Where'd he go?"

I shrugged. "Just disappeared, I guess."

"Disappeared," he repeated, his voice trailing off in thought. "You stay in here and don't go talking to no strangers." He took the root beer I handed him, popped it open as he walked back toward the car he was working on.

"I didn't say nothin' to him!" What Paw didn't realize was that I would've spoken to Knock if I had known he wasn't going to stick around long. I very much wanted to have a conversation with the man who'd held my fascination from the time I entered this world kicking and screaming. He was no stranger to me. No, not Knock. I welcomed his visit.

I said no more about Knock that day at the garage. I wandered out to where Paw lay head-first under a car on ramps. A large wrench clanked along the garage floor and slid toward my feet.

"Lulu!"

"Yeah, Paw?" I asked, bending down to find his face in the dark.

"Throw that in the toolbox, will ya? And will ya straighten up a little? There's a pile of dirty rags on the floor I need you to put in the bin."

Puzzled by his uncharacteristic desire to beautify the garage, I gathered greasy rags along the way and dropped the wrench into the open toolbox near the hood of the car. I held the rags to my nose and sniffed them one by one as I tossed them into the blue barrel in the corner of the garage. Earthy. Motor oil with the faintest odor of perspiration.

"Hey!" He yelled again, spotting my feet close by. "Go grab them folding chairs outta the back of my truck and tote them in here if you don't mind."

Now I was completely intrigued. Straightening the garage and bringing in chairs? For what? And where was Roy Boy when work needed to be done?

I climbed into the bed of Paw's pickup and, one by one, lowered the chairs over the side, dropping them into a pile on the ground. By the time the fifteenth chair was irreverently dropped onto the heap, I decided it was time to grab another Coke from the machine, which made it convenient for me to walk back past my father and satisfy my curiosity. Before any words came out of my mouth, Paw called out to me, "Take care of them chairs. They belong to the church."

I popped open my Coke and jumped out of the way of the bubbling foam spewing from the top of the can. "What's going on, Paw? Why do you have the church's chairs?"

"We're having a meeting."

"What kind of meeting?" I asked. "And who is that Marshall Law you were talkin' about last night with Mom? Is he the speaker?"

"Martial law ain't no person, Lulu. And you'll know what it is soon enough," he added under his breath. "It's grown-up stuff. Don't worry about it."

Worry? I'm not worried. Do I need to be?

"After you finish with them chairs, run on home and get cleaned up."

"Cleaned up? Do I have to go to your meeting? I thought you said it was a grown-up meeting?"

"Do as I say and tell Roy Boy to get cleaned up, too."

I looked forward to delivering that message to my brother and seeing the horrified look on his face when he learned he had to take a bath in the middle of the day. "Do I have to wear a dress?" I shuddered.

"No. Just want you to smell like a girl and not like a mechanic."

"What do you want Roy Boy to smell like?" I asked with dead silence coming back at me. My father didn't always appreciate my sense of humor.

After the chairs were carefully propped along the walls of the garage, I scurried home. I took the familiar path through my neighbor's yard and over the fence to my own backyard where I was joyfully attacked by the hulking mass of canine flesh we called Tippy, for obvious reasons. As if on queue, she toppled me like a bowling pin on league night.

Roy Boy took the news of an afternoon bath exactly as I expected. His plans of playing football with his friends had been thwarted, and I, being the bearer of the edict, got a swift kick to the shin when Mom wasn't looking.

"Roy E. the Eyor," I taunted. I was proud of my incredible ability to agitate my older brother, who had been unfortunate enough to inherit the family name "Pomeroy," or "Roy E., as he preferred being called. I was so happy that even his preferred name was not safe from my ridicule.

My given name, Effie Dee, could've been used as ammunition against me had I not learned to love it. My mother passed along her fascination with spelling games and word puzzles to me. When asked my name, I found it fun to say "Effie Dee" and explain that it was not spelled F-E-D. Even if the name had bothered me, I never would've let my brother know.

With the baths behind us, Mom, Roy Boy, and I walked to the garage to meet Paw who was putting his sparse housekeeping skills to work by sweeping up a year's accumulation of dirt and dust off the newly-vacant garage floor.

"Hey, Lulubelle, grab a rag and help me wipe up a little," Paw called to me.

"You wanted me to smell pretty," I reminded him.

"I didn't ask you to waller in grease. I just want you to wipe things down that look grimy."

"Paw? Now what did you say this meeting's about?" I looked at Mom and decided my chances of having my question answered was greater with her around.

He looked at Mom, who nodded her head and turned to dump ice into Paw's red hunting cooler. I waited as he gathered the words to say.

"Just some of us are concerned about having our rights taken away from us." He hesitated a minute to see if the answer would satisfy my curiosity, as he started arranging the chairs into a semicircle.

"What kinda rights?"

Paw rubbed the scruff on his chin and looked me in the eyes. "Well, the right to meetings, for one. And the right to have guns. And the right–"

Mom stamped her foot and shot Paw a look. "That's enough," she said. Her voice was much softer than her facial expression.

"Why would anyone wanna do that?" I asked, scratching myself furiously. "Why, Paw? "Why?"

"Effie, go get yourself something to drink, then go play," Mom suggested. "There's nothing for you to worry about."

There was that word again – worry. I still wasn't completely sure what Paw meant by "rights", but the part I did understand frightened me. I looked around for something to do while we waited for the others to arrive at the meeting. Paw pointed toward the clock hanging over the office door. Big hand on the twelve; little hand on the five. I ran to the front door and flipped the sign to the "Closed" side.

As I stood in the doorway, I saw Mr. Bantom pulling into the gravel lot. He walked in, shook Paw's hand and wiped his own on a paper towel before taking a cola out of the cooler. Paw didn't see him wipe his hand, but I did. Can't say that I blamed him too much since my Paw, Pomeroy Allen Whatley of Whatley's Garage, wasn't known to have the cleanest hands in town. Mom always said his hands were beautiful to her because they were hard-working hands – the more grease under his nails, the more money to pay the bills.

The sound of gravel crunching promised more visitors and beckoned me to look out to see who was arriving. I was happy to see the Derryhill family, specifically their son, Timmy, who was Roy Boy's age. They were followed by a young man, probably college-aged, who I didn't recognize, and a handful of other people I'd seen once or twice at the garage. Soon, nine of the chairs were occupied, and the room was full of small talk and chatter of politics. The young man sat back in his chair with his arms tightly folded across his chest, listening to an increasingly heated discussion between two of the older men.

Although I didn't know Timmy well, I gave Roy Boy a shove and told him to ask the Derryhills if he could play with us. He refused, so I decided to show him who was braver. I waltzed over to Mrs. Derryhill who seemed annoyed at first, but when I bent over and whispered in her ear, "Paw said the meeting might be long. Timmy will probably get very restless," she relented.

"As long as you don't touch any machinery, and stay away from the pit, and don't get dirty," she warned as she smoothed his hair and sent him on his way. She kept her eyes on Timmy as we took him across the garage to a corner where we explained the rules of our made-up game, "Hide the Wrench."

"It's gotta be somewhere on this side of the room, can't be mixed with any of Paw's other tools, and you can't touch no model cars. Paw will have a cow if you touch one of his model cars," I said firmly. "You go first, and we'll sit in the waiting room and count to 25."

As Roy Boy and I walked away, I turned to glance back at Mrs. Derryhill who looked worried that her son might get grease on his white button-down. I couldn't understand why she made him wear his good clothes to a greasy old garage, forgetting for a second that I, too, was forced to wear mine. As soon as we passed through the doorless entry to the waiting room, I began counting, "One, two, three, four, five . . ."

"Slow down!" Roy Boy shouted at me. "He's new. Give him a little more time. Now start over."

Mom turned in her chair toward us and put a finger up to her lips.

"One …….two……..three…….." slow enough, Eyor?" I goaded.

"Shut up and keep counting," he snapped.

"Four …………….five……………..six…….," I slowed more and more watching Roy Boy squirm in frustration.

"Don't be a—"

I frowned at him and pointed toward Paw's back office as a threat where I knew, and so did Roy Boy, a belt hung on the wall as a reminder to keep our mouths clean. Funny thing, Paw allowed us to hang around the garage with the mechanics, learning all the words we weren't allowed to say.

"Time's up. Let's go," Roy Boy announced before I

had a chance to complete my snail's- pace counting. I stuck my tongue out and made sure I jumped in front of him as we prepared to enter the garage.

"Whatever you say, Eyor," I mumbled back at him. "Ready or not, here we come!" I shouted, then covered my mouth when I saw Paw and Mrs. Derryhill giving me "the look" simultaneously.

I immediately ran to the rag bin and uncovered the wrench, holding it high into the air. "Ta-da!"

"You were looking when you shouldn't-a-been," Timmy said, his face downcast. He looked at Roy Boy who clearly didn't want to get in the middle of an argument between me and the defenseless Timmy.

"Did not. That's the first place everyone hides it when they ain't played before." Roy nodded in agreement. Mrs. Derryhill, who had been closely observing the exchange, frowned at me suspiciously, but I ignored her and told them to go count.

When the two of them were out of sight, I immediately stuck the wrench inside of Paw's empty thermos and screwed the lid back on. It was just barely tall enough to accommodate the wrench. I measured it earlier in the day in anticipation of this game. No one would ever want to touch the greasy-sided thing with dried soup dribbled down the side.

They came in looking over and under everything they could think of. As they searched, I took a seat on an overturned bucket and listened to the meeting.

"It's a nice, big piece of land," Mr. Bantom said. "With a wide creek and a decent cabin I use when I go hunting. Not luxurious living, but okay for a short while. There's a fireplace for heat. Also has another smaller cabin and nice, flat areas for tents."

"Sounds promising, Bantom," Paw said. It was odd to see Paw addressing a group, and I could tell he was nervous by the way he cleared his throat over and over.

"Only thing is you have to ford the creek to get to the property," Mr. Bantom continued.

"I'd say that makes it even better, don't you? Any fish in that creek?" Paw asked.

"Yeah. Pretty good fishin' if you go down to the deep part. It pools up right at the edge of my land."

"Who owns the land next to yours?" Paw asked.

"Don't know them personally. My buddy knows who they are, but says they never go up there. Never have seen hide nor hair of anyone in those woods. Trust me. It's isolated."

"Anyone have any other ideas or anything to say?" Paw inquired. "Then we all agree 'bout where it will be?"

Everyone looked around to the others and nodded. Roy Boy and Timmy were still fiercely determined to find the wrench. I smiled as they walked past the thermos which was sitting right out in plain sight. They looked under rugs, inside of boxes, everywhere except in the thermos next to Paw's toolbox.

The game was losing interest to me as I crouched on the bucket listening to discussions of firearms, food rations and shelters. I realized they were talking about a grown-up game of hide and seek. My intuition told me that my life was about to change, and my intuition was never wrong.

CHAPTER TWO

Roy Boy and I perched on the floor next to my parents' bed watching Paw fold work pants and place them inside the duffle bag which sat beside me. With each deposit he made into the stained canvas bag, the musty smell of weathered old tents and campfire smoke wafted into my face. I leaned my head closer and closer and drew in the fragrance, allowing it to transport me back to sweet summertime trips to the laurel-laden mountains just north of Burnt Willow. Me, Paw, and Roy Boy sitting out under the star-saturated sky, drinking hot cocoa as we roasted marshmallows on peeled hickory sticks. Paw scared us by telling ghost stories about bloody, headless mountain men. I remembered the sleepless nights, keeping vigil from my zipped sleeping bag, ready to pull my head completely inside should the tent suddenly open with a beastly face peering in.

"Why can't we go with you?" I asked.

"Lulu, hunting trips are no place for little girls. Besides, you've got school, and I'll be gone for a while."

He shoved a flannel shirt into the bag and struggled with the zipper until he managed to get it closed. "There. Don't reckon I can get anymore in this one. Let's go eat breakfast."

"How long will you be gone?"

"As long as it takes, Lulu."

"To kill something?" I asked.

Paw laughed and fluffed my hair. "Me and Mr. Bantom's got some repairs to get done."

I was puzzled. "On cars?"

"On his huntin' cabins."

"Ah, now I get it," I said. "Coming, Mom!"

Mom put Paw's plate down in front of him as he tucked his napkin into the top of his shirt. Eggs. Over easy. Just the way he always wanted them. Sprinkled with a little salt and pepper and topped with two dashes of Tabasco sauce.

"Roy Boy. Effie. Go take your bowls of oatmeal into the kitchen to eat. Paw and I need to talk."

I picked up my bowl and made sure I left the door to the dining room ajar so I could hear their conversation.

"I'm going to tell on you," Roy Boy said to me as I slid my chair closer to the door. I held a clenched fist to shush him. Of course, he obeyed. I could see the back of Mom's head as she sat quietly, watching Paw eat. When she did break the silence, I detected worry in her voice.

"How long will you be gone?"

"Can't tell exactly. Gotta make the cabins liveable. Make sure you get Lulubelle to that doctor while I'm gone."

"I'll make the appointment tomorrow if you think that's the best thing."

Roy Boy started humming loudly to keep me from

listening. I gave up and slid my chair back over to the small kitchen table.

"Ain't you worried?"

"'Bout what?" he asked.

"Worried about Paw being gone. Why does he have to repair some old cabins anyway?" Roy Boy shrugged and scraped the last of his oatmeal from the sides of his bowl.

I felt there was more to the story than we were being told. And what about that doctor's appointment? Maybe it was time for my booster shots? I couldn't ask Mom because she'd know I was listening. I scratched and waited for Mom and Paw to retrieve us from our kitchen banishment.

"Do you think Paw's really with the CIA and is on a secret mission? You know they can't tell their families where they are or what they're doing."

"Idiot," was his only reply.

I couldn't really picture Paw sleuthing around in some foreign country, spying on would-be assassins or some other undesirables. My gut feeling was that his suspicious hunting trips were more domestic in nature. But the strange thing was, he hadn't shot anything lately. Paw used to always come back with a deer. Was it even still hunting season?

They emerged from the dining room hand-in-hand. Paw let go of Mom's hand and held his arms out. We ran to him and were enveloped. I took a big sniff of his jacket sleeve.

A memory smell. Gasoline mixed with the smell clothing gets when it hangs outdoors.

"Bye, Lulubelle, Roy Boy," Paw said, still hugging me and my brother. "I'll be back before you know it."

I scratched a little more and watched as he drove off in his loaded-down pickup, leaving me to wonder about his mysterious hunting trip.

———————— • ● • ————————

Roy Sr. and Mr. Bantom tore at the woody vines as they walked toward a small, weathered cabin.

"This here is where I stay when I go huntin'," Bantom said. "It ain't much but it keeps the elements off of me. I think it could be fixed up real nice with a woman's touch. Kind of cozy. Enough space for the four of you. The man who owns it with me is always wantin' me to buy out his share. He's gettin' older now . . . well, older than me, and just doesn't use it much anymore. There's five acres that come along with it, and the people who own the adjacent property don't mind us cuttin' up through it to get here. I hear they're holdin' out hopes that someone will come in here and want to purchase all the land for a resort or a hunting lodge or something." Banton laughed. "I believe they're gonna be waitin' a long time!"

Roy Sr. sheltered his eyes and looked to the right, then left a couple of times and said, "I think it'll work out just fine. Lots of flat land for a garden in that clearing over there. You said the wildlife makes good huntin'. Nice and private, that's for sure. That's the most important thing. We don't want no one findin' us. Yeh, I think it'll work just fine."

"Good. Now, you know I trust you and what you've told me about the problems coming. So, Whatley, I don't mind financing this whole thing if it's for our own good, but I can't help but worry a little bit. What if this thing blows over and there's no trouble? I know, I know, you've given me your assurance, but I'm puttin' a whole lot of trust in you, not to mention a whole lot of money. That's why I'm going to have to get you to sign a promissory note for half the cost if this ends up being a wild goose chase. Sorry 'bout that. It's just good business."

Roy Sr. sighed, bowed his head and muttered, "You know I ain't got much money, Bantom, but maybe I can come up with it somehow."

"Sorry to have to do this, Roy, but you and I go back pretty far and, well, I don't mean this to sound insulting but you haven't always been the sharpest tack in the box when it comes to financial deals," he chuckled. "You've had your share of failures before hittin' on this garage business of yours. You've got yourself a pretty nice little thing going, and I'm happy for you." Bantom rubbed his brow and knocked a small stone out of the hard ground with the side of his boot before continuing.

"What about givin' me your garage if this whole hideout ordeal don't amount to anything? It's the only collateral you have. If you're right, you've got nothing to worry about." Roy remained silent as Bantom continued, "I hate to do this, but I gotta protect myself. I'll be investin' quite a bit of money. There's the cost of the property and building materials. Worst case scenario, you might lose your garage, but you'll have a nice place to go huntin' anytime you wish. What do you think?"

Roy squinted and looked away, his eyes scoped the surroundings before turning back toward Bantom. He held out his hand. Bantom shook it and patted him on the back.

"You've heard the same reports I've heard, Bantom. The government's gonna come after everything we have when gasoline's hard to get. That means your fancy gun collection and ammo, too. You're bringin' all that with you up to the camp, right?"

Bantom nodded. "Worried about what Vinca will say? Do you wanna talk it over with her before making it final? I can give you a day or two to think."

"Vinca ain't gonna like it, for sure. She can't hear anything about this, okay? It's my decision. I've put that woman through a lot and, well, no tellin' what she'd do if she found out."

Bantom nodded again. "Mum's the word. But she'll find out if things don't go so good. Just know that you'll always have a job waiting for you at the garage. I want you to be able to care for your family."

"Bantom, you know I'm a Christian man, but there might be a little lyin' involved. We don't wanna scare the kids. We gotta make them think this is a fun time. Vinca and the other grown-ups know there's government trouble coming, but we don't want them panicking. So when bad things start happening back home, we need to protect them and make them feel safe. Let's shelter the women and children as much as we can. Agreed?"

"I completely understand. But why did you invite the others to come along? I know the Derryhills are friends, but what about Chris and that young couple? Why them?" Bantom asked.

"We need strong backs. There's a lot of hard work to do and the two of us can't handle it all. I've had some good talks with Chris. He's a big hiker and knows the woods pretty well. I guess he blabbed to the married couple. I suppose that's okay. They're friends of his, and he needs to have friends his age at the camp. It'll keep him happy."

Bantom nodded. "Good thinkin'. Roy, we're dependin' on you and your survival know-how."

"I know what I'm doin'." Roy pulled a rag out of his back pocket and wiped his forehead.

"A little worried, are you Roy? You look nervous." Bantom asked.

"Just hotter than blazes out here. That's all," Roy replied.

Bantom chuckled and popped Roy on the arm. "You got nothin' to worry about. Just show up at Bob Smithgall's office in the morning and we'll sign those papers. Just a formality, Roy. Nothin' against you, my friend."

"I'll be there."

CHAPTER THREE

On Thursday, I was taken to visit Dr. Carlton, a lady doctor I'd never laid eyes on before. She had no needles or scary-looking things sitting around like my regular doctor. She had me sit down and play with some dolls as she asked me strange questions about my friends and Knock. I'm not sure how she knew about Knock, but I loved talking about him. It bothered me, however, that she kept referring to him as my make-believe friend.

"Ain't you gonna give me a shot or anything?"

"No," she replied with a smile. "This is just a getting-acquainted visit. No shots and no medicine. Bet you're glad about that!"

"Yeah. Real glad. Then what's wrong with me? I don't feel sick or nothing."

"There's nothing wrong with you, honey." Dr. Carlton touched my shoulder and opened the door, leading me back to the room where Mom waited.

"Your turn, Mom," she said. "Effie, you go read the books in the basket while your Mom and I talk for a few minutes."

Mom winked at me. "See you shortly. I'll be right in here if you need me."

I was confused. Curiosity got the best of me, so I mashed my ear up against the door and listened carefully, trying to figure out what was going on. I was glad Roy Boy wasn't around to squeal on me.

I heard Dr. Carlton explain to Mom that children don't usually have memories of anything that happened to them before their fifth birthday, so my stories about Knock visiting me as a baby were highly unlikely. She used phrases like "anxiety, and "normal part of childhood", and "a way of dealing with changes in her life." In her low smoky voice, the doctor assured my mother that Knock would fade away over time.

On our way home from the appointment, I told Mom what I knew she wanted to hear.

"Guess the doctor's right. Guess Knock is make-believe. 'Spose I made him up from some dream I had when I was a kid." I kept my crossed fingers tucked under my legs, out of sight. Upon telling this lie, I felt sure his name would then be allowed to pass through my lips without the worried looks I'd grown accustomed to seeing on my parents' faces.

At the first stop sign, Mom turned toward me and smiled, saying nothing. She looked like she wanted to say something, but kept silent.

"Can I still pretend about him, Mom?" She nodded.

From this time on, I knew Knock would be accepted as part of the family, albeit a distant relative who could only be reached via my newly-deemed anxious mind. I knew better, and I suspected my mother was not one hundred percent convinced by the doctor that Knock was a childhood fantasy that would be driven away by my advancing age like the boogie man and Santa Claus. She kept her thoughts hidden, and I suspected she would continue to do so, especially around Paw.

The following day, when I arrived home from school, Paw was on the front porch waiting for Roy Boy and me to get off the bus. I ran and jumped into his arms. He spun me around and tousled my short brown hair with his rough fingers. Next, he hoisted Roy Boy with a loud grunt and set him down gently.

"Whew! Won't be able to do that much longer! Why, you musta put on a few pounds since I saw you last," he said, pretending to wipe sweat from his brow.

"Catch anything, Paw? Any deer?"

"No, Lulu. 'Fraid not."

I looked at Roy Boy and made a "told you so" look. He ignored me.

"We're gonna have a cookout tonight," Paw announced. "And I have a surprise to tell you about later. Now go get your homework done and leave me and your Mom to get dinner stuff ready. We're gonna eat picnic-style outside."

Paw grabbed another hot dog off the plate and held the bowl of potato salad to Mom, who shook her head and patted her stomach. "How do you like them hot dogs?" he asked, wiping a smear of mustard off the corner of his mouth.

"I like 'em a lot!" Roy Boy said.

Paw looked at me and raised his eyebrows. "What

about you, Lulubelle?"

"Pretty good, I reckon." I answered as I brushed a flying bug out of my face. "Why'd you cook 'em on the grill? Mom usually boils 'em."

"Wanted to try out my new grill. Going to be doing a lot of grilling soon," he answered.

I wanted to be excited but the plastic smile on Mom's face led me to believe this had something to do with the surprise Paw talked about earlier. I worried that the surprise wasn't going to be one of those jump up and down, "yippee", fun surprises. I looked at Roy Boy whose face was aglow – gullible, as usual.

Paw chewed the last bite of his half-burnt hot dog and swallowed hard. "Now I'm going to tell you the secret I've been keeping." He smiled at the three of us and continued. "I've been fixin' up a little place and thought we could all spend some time there when school's out."

Mom smiled at me and Roy Boy, who clapped his hands together and jumped out of his chair. I studied Mom's face for any evidence of concern. She seemed calm enough.

"Where? Mr. Bantom's huntin' cabin?" I asked. I didn't think it would be polite to ask "why" yet, although I wondered why we'd want to spend time there after Paw told me it wasn't any place for little girls.

"Yep. Just a little north of here toward the mountains."

"Can we go hikin' and fishin', Paw?" Roy Boy asked, his eyes bulging with excitement.

"There'll be lots of hikin' and fishin', son. As much as you want."

In Roy Boy's excitement, he knocked over his glass of milk. Mom rose to grab the dish towel hanging from the handle of the grill.

"How long are we gonna stay?" I asked, jumping out of the way of the milk that was creeping close to the edge of the table.

"A while."

"Your Paw needs time to rest. He never gets a vacation," Mom added as she sopped-up Roy Boy's mess.

"So, this is vacation?" A bit of relief came over me although no one answered me back.

"It'll be a lot of fun and a real good learning experience for you two kids." She collected the ketchup and mustard and headed into the kitchen.

I held up the stub of my hot dog and shoved the bite I was chewing over into my cheek so I could speak. "Fine job on the hot dogs, Paw. Real Fine." I figured I'd better get used to eating a lot of grilled hot dogs. Paw seemed eager to cook out on our vacation. I had to admit, I did like the smell of a charcoal grill.

Mom furiously canned fruits and vegetables over the next few weeks while Paw was away with Mr. Bantom. I loved opening the pantry door to admire the rainbow she created on the shelves – green jars on the top shelf, reds and yellows on the next shelf down. On the bottom, were mason jars filled with multi-colored relishes and purple jams and jellies. I bent down and breathed-in the sweet, minty aroma of herbs from the bags that were wedged under the bottom shelf. Each bag was carefully labeled with the ingredient's botanical name and its use. Mom loved her herbal tea and believed in the healing properties each plant possessed. She saw me fingering the bags and peeped over the top of her reading glasses.

"I can handle just about any kind of ailment you kids could possibly come down with while we're in the woods," she said as she continued writing. Mom had nearly completed compiling a reference notebook of herbal remedies. She shut the white, three-ring binder and labeled it "Vinca's Herbal Reference".

"Why do you have so much of this stuff, Mom?"

"We might be needing it."

"We ain't needed this much before."

"Haven't ever," Mom corrected. "And don't sass me."

I didn't think my comment was sassy, but I held my tongue. Mom had seemed a little short-tempered lately and had been quick to grab the fly swatter off the kitchen wall to whack my legs over the slightest thing. Paw's absence clearly affected all of us. He would come home for a day or two, fix a car, then take off again with the clothes Mom washed for him.

"I've got to get this soap started. So much to do. So much to do . . ." her voice drifted off as she crossed the kitchen and pulled out her canister of Crisco.

"You mean people can make soap?" I asked.

Mom chuckled. "It doesn't grow on trees!"

"Can't you just buy it at the store?"

"There won't be any markets where we're going. I'll buy some to get us started until my homemade soap has cured properly."

I watched as Mom mixed the steaming lye solution.

"Stay far back. This stuff will hurt you," she warned. "I'll let you stir the other pot."

I sat up high on a stool and slowly stirred the thick Crisco into the shiny oils over and over until Mom said the thermometer read just the right temperature for combining with the lye.

She blended the two together as it turned to a pudding-like consistency. She poured in two tablespoons of fragrant oils – lavender and rose – until its heavenly bouquet filled the kitchen. In a figure eight pattern, she continued stirring until she gave me the signal, which meant I needed to bring her the cup of lavender blossoms she had placed on the kitchen counter. She nodded. "It's time, Effie."

I scrambled to pick up the cup and sprinkled it into the delightful porridge. Around and around Mom stirred until all the blossoms disappeared into the liquid soap.

"Why do you put flowers in it?"

"To make it special," was her answer. "We girls need to feel pampered a little, especially while we're in the woods."

"Are we gonna take baths? Paw never makes me take a bath when we go camping."

"You're gonna have me there this time, so there'll be lots of bathing. No bathtub, but we'll have showers."

I was enraptured as Mom poured the mixture into the greased molds and covered them with paper towels to keep the dust out throughout the curing process.

After the soap molds were stored away in the laundry room, I flipped through the book Mom had sitting on the kitchen counter, *Surviving in the Woods*. She had dog-eared some pages, so I turned to those and studied the interesting folk skills that were displayed. Cheese-making, candle-dipping, foraging for edible plants. I found the sections on butchering animals terribly disturbing and hoped this wasn't anything I'd ever witness in my lifetime. *Could*

Mom really do that to a cute little animal?

Later that evening, Paw came walking through the door and announced that it was getting close to the time when we would leave. There would be one more trip to the "camp", as he now called it, to take supplies. Through the conversations he had with Mom, I determined we were not going on vacation by ourselves but would be joined by several others. Mr. Bantom seemed to be a given. The Derryhills were mentioned, along with someone named Chris. Before Paw left this final time, we were instructed to pack up only the essential items for day-to-day life and have them ready for loading in the car in one week's time, the day after school was out for summer break.

"What are essentials?" I asked Mom.

"Essentials are things you can't live without." Mom opened the bag I had already begun packing for vacation and pulled out two jigsaw puzzles.

"I gotta have something to play with."

"Effie, you'll have a creek to play and fish in. There'll be Tippy to play with, and of course, your brother. I think you'll find plenty to keep yourselves busy without dragging along everything from your closet."

"But we need games."

"We'll play games. Family games we can all play together like Charades. Your Paw loves Charades."

I was confused. "My Paw? I've never seen him play anything except touch football and tag. You mean Paw will actually play games like that with us? He's always so tired."

Then Mom threw a shocker at us. "Your Paw won't be going to work for a while after we leave, so he should be nice and rested."

My heart pounded. "I don't understand. Is there something wrong with him?' I rubbed my arms vigorously. *Don't scratch. Don't scratch.* I wanted to but didn't.

"Nope. He's fine, Honey. Don't worry. He just thinks we need an adventure."

"We are coming back, aren't we?" The itch was unbearable. I was starting to feel like this was not going to be a normal vacation.

"We'll be back," Mom said, not making eye contact with me. "Before you know it, we'll be back." I detected sadness in her expression and felt that I now understood why she packed box after box of supplies. I sensed the whole truth would be too painful to hear. Blasted intuition.

Our essentials were packed, as instructed, and lay piled in stacks by the back door. We each left one box open for last minute items. Mom relented and allowed us to stuff one box as full as we could with toys and puzzles. Unfortunately, she told us we would have to share these things with Timmy. I opened the lid to my unfinished box when no one was around and slid my fingers under the clothes until they met their intended, furry target. Bear-Bear was off limits and would not be shared with Timmy no matter what Mom said. I would rather risk her disappointment with my selfishness than to share him with anyone. He was mine, and mine alone.

I positioned myself in a corner and began the act of committing another violation – the smuggling of unauthorized contraband. I took a pack of Juicy Fruit gum out of my shirt pocket and shoved it into Bear-Bear's little yellow pants. I reached back into my pocket and quickly snatched the spearmint gum out and slid it in as well. I'd been saving them for a special occasion.

We heard that Paw was home this past week but didn't see much evidence of it. He slept at the house each night but was gone every morning by the time Roy Boy and I were up. On Friday evening, we were thrilled when he came through the front door just as Mom told us "good night." He collapsed into his easy chair, kicked off his grimy shoes and flopped his feet onto the coffee table. He felt hot and sweaty as I wrapped my arms around his neck.

"You kids, go on to bed. I'm tired."

Roy Boy and I kissed him "goodnight".

"Vinca? Are you gonna be up for a while?" he called to Mom.

"I'm gonna finish cleaning the kitchen," I heard her tell Paw. Then her voice got quieter. "We're doing the right thing," she said over and over to herself. "It'll all work out for the best."

I found the gentle clanking and light shuffling sounds in the kitchen comforting as I lay awake, anxious because I knew the event we'd been packing for was coming soon. I must've fallen off to sleep at some point. I distinctly remember strange dreams about Paw. Only he didn't look like Paw. He looked like a thinner, older version of Paw, but his voice was the same. "Don't forget me," the old man said as he walked away down a road. The very next thing I remember is Mom's voice saying my name softly.

"Effie?"

I felt a gentle pat on my leg, opened my bleary eyes to see Mom's silhouette in the glow of my nightlight.

"Time to get up, Sweetie."

"What time is it?" I asked, looking toward my

darkened window.

"Very early, but Paw said it's time to leave."

I felt that all-too-familiar lump in my stomach. It seemed like a cruel trick, waking me to face such a big change in my life. Somehow, though, it didn't completely surprise me to be getting up in the wee hours. Surprise was the new norm in my life.

CHAPTER FOUR

We bounced down a dirt road for what seemed like forever before pulling under a canopy of trees. Paw parked the car, turned to the back seat and looked straight at Roy Boy and me. A smile lightened his face. Odd, since he wasn't too overly fond of smiling.

"We're almost there." He paused and looked at Mom for her reaction. She quietly nodded and twisted to the right and left, surveying the surrounding forest, which had turned soft and misty in the growing sunlight.

"We're gonna leave the car here and hike the rest of the way. The other men and I will carry the gear to the camp. You three just need to follow me." Paw slung a pair of rubber gaiters over his shoulder.

"Shouldn't we lock the car doors?" My question was met with laughter from Mom and Paw. I didn't think I'd said anything funny.

"Lulu, you worry too much. No one's gonna bother nothin' out here. A bear, maybe, but no human. Go ahead and lock 'em if it'll make you feel better," Paw said. "On second thought, Mr. Bantom and Chris will be along soon and will need to get stuff out of the car, so leave 'em unlocked."

I turned to look at the car several times as we walked away through the thickening trees. It saddened me to see it looking lonely and vulnerable in that unfamiliar place. Soon the car was completely out of sight and my attention was on Paw as he pointed out things to avoid in the woods.

"See them three leaves on that plant? That's poison ivy. We've got us a little of that around the back of the shop back home, but you're gonna see a lot of it out here. You don't want to touch that stuff. It'll itch the fire outta ya."

We headed down a slight incline and came to a wide creek. Moss-covered rocks flanked one side of it. Thick brown brush lined the other. There was a small opening in the brush across the creek, which seemed like it may have been cleared by someone. Roy Boy and I looked at each other, puzzled. Paw walked to the water's edge and studied the rocks for a moment before speaking.

"Come on down here and keep your shoes on so you don't cut your feet. Don't be afraid. I'll help each of you through the water. Roy Boy, why don't you go first?" Paw called out as he slipped his tall boots on.

Roy Boy looked stricken with fear and shook his head, staring straight ahead at Paw.

"Weiner," I mumbled at him. "I'll do it, Paw!" I had my shoes off before anyone could protest. I loved the water, but I loved showing up Roy Boy better. I ran to where Paw stood and peeked back over my shoulder at Roy Boy. "Are you sure there ain't any snakes, Paw?" I whispered.

Paw shrugged. "Don't know," was his honest answer.

"Might be too cool for them, but I just don't know."

Determined not to let my fear show and, of course, not to back down in front of Roy Boy, I sucked in an earthy fresh breath, dipped my foot in the creek and quickly withdrew it as my shoe filled up. Tippy stood next to me and slurped up the glistening water.

"Cold, Paw." I delayed for a few moments and looked around for any sign of snakes.

"It'll only reach up to your knees, Lulubelle. So just stick both feet in and run." The creek sparkled its way around Paw's legs as he stood in front of me, waiting.

"She's scared!" Roy Boy blurted. He must've forgotten how he backed out of going first.

I took that comment as a dare, grabbed Paw's hand and ran off hopping through the swift, frigid water as rapidly as I could without slipping on the smooth river rocks. I glared at Roy Boy from the other side.

"Run as fast as you can, and you won't even feel the water! It's easy!" I yelled to him. This wasn't entirely true. In fact, it wasn't true at all. The cold water cut like a knife, and I nearly slipped two times on the slick rocks before reaching the bank on the other side.

I exploded in delight as Roy Boy took off like a dragster on Saturday night, tumbling on the first rock he hit. Paw pulled him to his feet and led him back to where Mom waited with a blanket.

"You okay?" I half-heartedly called out. "You've gotta be careful, Roy Boy!"

I could tell he wanted to cry as Mom wrapped his shaking, dripping body in the blanket. Paw scooped up the bundled Roy Boy and carried him across the current, gently depositing him next to me on the creek's bank.

"You'll do better next time," I patronized, patting him on his arm. "Just watch out for snakes. The place is crawlin' with 'em. Paw told me so."

"I hope one bites you," he mumbled, as we watched Mom roll her pants legs up, preparing for the crossing. I stuck my tongue out at him.

"Be careful, Mom! Them rocks are real slippery! If you run, you'll fall like Roy Boy!"

Mom stepped into the water and shrieked. "You didn't warn me that it was so cold!"

Paw laughed and stepped in front of Mom with his back facing her. "Hop on."

Mom lifted one leg and Paw grabbed the other as she clutched his shoulders tightly. It was a strange sight to see Paw and Mom being playful. I was amazed by the exhibition of Paw's strength, as well. Mom was not a small woman, and Paw hoisted her up like he was picking up ten pounds of gasoline.

We all began calling to Tippy, who was barking at us from the water's edge.

"Come on, Tippy! Come on!"

"If I can do it, you can, too!" Roy Boy shouted. I started to remind him that he didn't really do it but saved my comments. He'd suffered enough.

Tippy continued barking, dipping one paw in, then the other. We continued encouraging him as he walked into the water up to his shoulders and began paddling, being carried slightly downstream by the swift current. He had not chosen the shallow, rocky path across. Paw stepped out a little from the shore and grabbed the dog by the collar and led him to where we sat. Tippy shook, sending water flying over us. We collected the few things we had carried from the car.

"Okay, everyone. Get up and follow me. We'll be there soon," Paw said, lending Mom a hand as she rose. "Now stay close. You don't know these woods yet."

We lined up behind Paw like a row of ducklings – Mom, followed by Roy Boy wrapped like an Indian in a blanket, then me and Tippy bringing up the rear. Our wet shoes squished as we tramped through the clearing between thick walls of evergreens and mountain laurel.

"Bantom and me, we cleared a mess of trees and brush so we could move our stuff in. We dragged lumber and roofing material up that path with his equipment. Used to be a logging road, I reckon." Paw said, pointing toward a rugged trail. "We blocked that path off by putting a bunch of brush in the way to disguise it. We actually had to construct a little bridge over that creek to get the stuff across, but it got washed away after a heavy rainstorm. Good thing it lasted as long as it did or we couldn't have done all our work," Paw said as he trudged along. "We hoped it would last long enough to get everyone across, then we were gonna tear it down for our protection against intruders. Bantom's gonna use a long 2X4 to slide stuff across later."

"We made the path we're on just for walking. It twists a lot, so watch your step." He pushed a sagging limb out of the way and continued up the path. Paw seemed in his element. He jabbered the entire way through the woods, taking shorts breaks only to turn around and grab Mom's hand or give her a quick peck on the cheek. Mom clearly looked like she enjoyed the change in Paw. I'd never heard him talk so much. Where did he learn so much about the trees, weather signs, and woodland animals? He loved the out-of-doors, but I never knew he was this knowledgeable about anything except car engines. And I'd never seen him show this much enthusiasm over them.

We turned yet another direction on our hike. Paw did an about-face toward us and stopped.

"Y'all stay here for a few minutes. I'll be right back. You'll be okay," he said, looking at my panicked expression. I clutched Mom's arm.

"I just need to go and make sure everything's ready for you." He left us and went over a small rise, disappearing from sight. The early morning sun shot rays between the pines on the horizon, causing me to squint as I watched for Paw's return. When Paw's "few minutes" turned into a long time, Roy Boy and I started exploring the immediate area, afraid to venture too far from Mom. From a large rock, I could see part of the way down the path we had just climbed.

"Look at that funny tree!" I yelled to Mom, who was taking a sip of water from her canteen. At the side of the path stood two large oaks, joined at the base for roughly five feet before separating. The base was broad with a giant gnarled root protruding outward. A thick, ropy vine crawled its way around and around toward the top branches.

"Well, how about that?" Mom said. "That's a marrying tree. My Aunt Thressie used to tell me that it's good luck to tell a marrying tree all of your secrets about a boy you like, then someday, he'll ask you to marry him. See how it's joined at the base and spreads its arms up to the sky? It's just like being married. You're two people, but at the base you're joined as one, reaching up toward God, Who waters you and feeds you."

I gazed up through the branches of this marvelous marrying tree. Its bright green leaves flapped in the gentle breeze like fans waving us a welcoming greeting.

"And I guess that big old root coming out is kinda like me? You all keep me sheltered under your branches." I was impressed with my poetic comment.

"Suppose it could be like that," Mom said. "Except I think maybe you're more like that little sapling trying to sprout out of that acorn over there." She tapped the acorn slightly with her toe.

"Yeah." I agreed. "I guess that's better than the root thing I said. And that poison whatever-it-is crawling up the trunk would be like Roy Boy. You shouldn't touch him 'cause you might catch something itchy." I grinned at my older brother who was acting like he didn't hear. He reached down, picked up the acorn-sapling and chucked it as far as he could downhill.

"Much better," he said, wiping off his hands. "Too bad you had to go away."

I turned to stick my tongue out at him, but Paw appeared over the hilltop. He dashed down the uneven path, stumbling slightly as he approached us.

"Follow me." We did, and soon saw a clearing with a couple of ramshackle cabins and two more small frames for future structures.

"Welcome home," Paw said, studying our faces for a reaction.

"Home?" Roy Boy and I said in unison.

"We're gonna live here?" my stunned-faced brother

asked. Paw nodded. "For how long?"

"As long as we have to, but not forever," Mom said.

"You mean until school starts, right?" I asked.

Paw looked at Mom, who looked back at him with an expression that said, "Your turn to answer."

"Well. We'll see," was all he said, and I didn't like the way he said it.

"What are we gonna eat?" I wondered as my stomach growled its displeasure over the thought of missing my morning bowl of Frosty-Os.

"You'll eat better than you've ever eaten before. Your Mom has fixed up some real good stuff in jars. And we'll have lots of cookouts. You like cookouts, don't you?" Roy Boy and I nodded.

"Let's quit talking, and I'll show you around." Paw took my hand and led us all to the first cabin. "This one's ours." He pushed the door open, and I immediately noticed how dark it was inside. I tentatively peered inside the cabin, not wanting to step through the door by myself. Spiders lived there. I was sure.

"Wait just a moment! I almost forgot!" Paw swept Mom up into his arms and carried her through the doorway and set her down in that dark room. She laughed. How could she be so happy about being in the dark spider room?

"We're not newlyweds!" She chuckled. "And we've got them to prove it. Remember?" She laughed again and squeezed Paw's waist.

"Don't matter. It's the beginning of a new life for us."

New life? But I don't want a new life. There wasn't anything wrong with the old one.

CHAPTER FIVE

Throughout the course of the day, the men made trips back down the trail to gather and tote the packed supplies. I noticed a never-ending caravan of Derryhill boxes. *So much for packing just the essentials.* It didn't seem fair to me that we'd been restricted to one box each of fun stuff when I know I saw four or five boxes marked "Timmy's Things" in big black letters.

"Guess we don't need to share our stuff with him," I said to Roy Boy as we watched the Derryhill's pile grow larger and larger.

"We'll all share as needed," Mom corrected.

I could tell by the look on her face she was thinking the same thing I was, however.

With one more trip down the hill everything was here. One stack was marked "FOOD SUPPLIES"; one grouping of boxes was ours; one belonged to Mr. Bantom; one for Mr. Chris; one for a young married couple named "O'Neil"; and finally, there was a heaping mound for the Derryhills.

"Let's get this stuff covered," Mr. Bantom said,

looking at the sky. "We need to tarp up those two houses over there and get them ready for living in."

I looked at the open, framed structures across the property and wondered who would be sleeping there. Probably no spiders. Why couldn't we live in one of those places?

Out of a giant duffel bag, the men unpacked a tarp larger than any I'd ever seen. Mr. Chris climbed a ladder and shimmied to the top of the first structure, bent over and grabbed the tarp as Paw lifted it to him.

When Mr. Chris got the edge of the tarp halfway across the top, he attached twine to the grommets and lowered the strings to the men on the ground, who pulled the tarp across the remainder of the roof and down the exposed side. This left only the front and back of the "cabin" open.

"At least they'll be protected from the elements temporarily. One more to go, men," Mr. Bantom said, and the process was repeated on the next building.

I loved watching Mr. Chris crawl across the beams like a circus performer. His wavy blond hair hung across his sweaty brow like a golden crown reminding me of the prince in my Cinderella book. He was the most handsome grown-up I'd ever seen.

"Lulu!" Paw called out. "Go grab us some water from the cooler. The cups are in that yellow bag."

"Yes, Paw!" I yelled back. I ran to the big red cooler and scooped some ice into five cups and poured water from the large canteen which had been kept cool atop the ice. Little did I know ice would become a thing of the past. A treasured commodity I would only dream about.

I carried the first two cups to the men, sloshing only a

little bit out along the way. I handed Mr. Chris the first cup. After all, he did all of the climbing.

"Thanks, Effie," he said in a soft tenor voice.

"You're welcome!" I chirped back. "Let me know if I can get you some more!"

"Here, Paw." I handed Paw my next cup. "Sorry about the muddy fingerprints."

I stood watching them drink, hoping Mr. Chris would ask for more.

"Lulubelle. Don't forget the other men."

"Right, Paw!" I ran back to the cooler and grabbed two more cups of water and took them to Mr. Bantom and Mr. Derryhill.

"I'll be right back with yours!" I said to Mr. Mike (although I wasn't certain of his name at the time).

"Now go help the women unpack the food. We're gonna be hungry after we get this job done," Paw said to me. He probably wanted me to go away and stop staring at Mr. Chris.

I reluctantly went to where Mom and the others were unwrapping the egg salad sandwiches and placing them on paper plates. Timmy doled out potato chips.

"Shouldn't Timmy and Roy Boy be over there helping the men?" My comment was met with a shocked expression from Mrs. Derryhill. Mom gave me a "keep your big mouth shut" look.

"I just thought since they're boys and we're girls, they'd . . ." I knew it was time to heed Mom's warning and not cause Mrs. Derryhill to blow a gasket, for whatever reason. "I'll go tell them it's time to eat."

Mom nodded, so I ran off to where the men unfolded

cots to go inside the tent-cabins.

"Who's sleeping there?" I asked, pointing at one of the tarped homes.

"Probably Bantom and Chris. Or maybe Mike and Michelle," Paw answered.

"Looks like fun! Like camping!"

"It'll be fun until the mosquitos chew them up or the cold weather comes in. But by that time, we'll have them all finished with real walls."

"But it won't get cold for a long time, Paw. We'll be gone by then." Paw was silent. I looked away and knew not to pursue it further.

"Oh. Lunch is ready. By the way, you did a good job climbing, Mr. Chris. I bet it was real scary."

He smiled. "Not at all. I like climbing. I used to climb a lot of trees when I was about your age."

The women cleaned up the lunch trash and started putting away the supplies for the next week, while the men sat in a circle under a tree discussing the projects to be done immediately.

All of the boxes were marked with "to be used by" dates. I asked Mom why, since we weren't going to be here for very long . . . or so I believed.

"Well, we aren't very self-sufficient yet," Mom explained. "We need more supplies until we have our own produce and meat." She told me that we would be living off the land best we could. I was terribly afraid that included doing things I remembered seeing in some of her books. Poor animals.

Paw whistled and waved his arms above his head, beckoning everyone to come to where he stood.

"Meetin' time will be at 7:00 each night in my cabin for everyone. After the youngins are in bed, we grown-ups will meet again at 8:30 over at Bantom's place to go over stuff."

"Why two meetings?" Mr. Derryhill asked.

"The first meetin' will be our devotion time, and time for the kids to ask whatever they want. It won't take long. The second one will be to talk about work we need to do and other stuff that don't concern the kids. There's a lot to get done. I'll be checkin' the radio news out every night before I go to bed. If there's anything to report, I'll let you know at the grown-ups' meetin'."

Mr. Derryhill seemed satisfied with Paw's answer, but I noticed a sour expression on Mr. Chris' face.

"We're all a big family now and need to work together. You guys were told it would be hard," Paw said. Mr. Chris looked up and nodded.

"You also knew there'd be lots of things expected of ya, so go on now and get started unpackin' your gear."

I couldn't believe the change that had come over Paw. Back home, Mom was always the one who laid down the law, or maybe it just seemed that way because Paw was gone so much. He would come home from the garage and flop, saying almost nothing all evening. Now the roles had changed and both of them seemed so content.

Mom headed into the cabin, so I reluctantly followed after her.

"Will I really have to be in bed by 8:30?" I asked. "We never had to go to bed early before when we went camping."

"I have a feeling you'll be so tuckered out you'll want

to go to bed even sooner than 8:30," she replied. "And there isn't any TV or record players to entertain you."

Mom shined her flashlight into the corners of the cabin where the stream of sunlight couldn't reach, walked to a window and opened it.

"Needs some airing out," she said as she crossed the cabin to the other window.

"'Spose there's lots of spiders in here?" I asked.

"Maybe. But you're in the woods now, so you'd better get used to all the bugs. And animals."

"Thanks for makin' me feel better." I scratched my arm and followed the beam of Mom's flashlight with my eyes. The part about the animals, I didn't mind. But bugs, I could do without. I'd watched the movie *The Fly* with Roy Boy once and decided that spiders must be the most horrifying creature God ever created.

Roy Boy walked into the cabin with a large stick in his hands, which he propped against the wall near the front door.

"Effie, I need you and Roy Boy to carry in all the boxes that say "bedroom" on them. We need to get the beds made and ready for tonight." Mom knocked cobwebs off the ceiling with a broom as Roy Boy and I walked out into the bright sunlight to locate our bedroom boxes.

"Are you scared?" I asked my brother.

"Of what?"

"Livin' here."

"It's just like camping. Camping didn't scare you."

"Camping was camping, but this is livin'. And what about the spiders and stuff?" I needed reassurance from him that there was nothing to be afraid of.

"Be quiet and get to work," he replied.

"I think I'll sleep out under the stars. You can sleep inside the cabin." I dropped the first box on the cabin's front step.

"Chicken," Roy Boy muttered. "Don't go leaving that box sitting there."

"Who died and made you my boss, Eyor?"

I picked up the box and followed him through the front door. Mom was busy unpacking the vegetables she'd canned, carefully placing them on some wooden shelves in the kitchen.

"How come we got the big cabin?" I asked her.

"Because we're the biggest family. The Derryhills got the next biggest because they're the second biggest family. Mr. Bantom said he wanted the families to have privacy."

Mom placed a row of canisters on the kitchen counter. I noticed that they were all labeled with the herb's name and medicinal use. I opened each one and drew in the aroma.

"Um. Yummy. This one's my favorite," I said, tapping the one labeled "spearmint". I loved that smell. It reminded me of chewing gum.

"Very good choice," Mom said, as she dipped sugar out of a large bag and poured it into a fancy glass jar.

"No. I take that back. That's my favorite!" I said, licking my fingers and catching each crystal that dropped from her spoon onto the counter.

"Stay out of it, Effie. Might be a while before we can replenish our supply."

Our first day at the camp went by quickly. After dinner, there was time for a short touch football game before the earliest meeting. Timmy sat on the sidelines looking miserable, next to his mother who was reading a romance novel. Tippy joined in the fun by tackling anyone who got close enough to where he happened to be at the time. His massive tongue hung from his mouth, dripping saliva, as he panted.

Paw retreated to the cabin and emerged with his Bible and a piece of notebook paper in his hand. He motioned for everyone to join him inside and we all ambled our way behind him, each flopping onto the floor out of exhaustion. All except Timmy and Mrs. Derryhill, who pulled up chairs to sit on.

Paw's pained expression reminded me of the way he looked when he had a toothache last year. He fidgeted and fumbled and twisted that piece of notebook paper into a tight tube before finally sitting.

"'Spose we orta pray," he said, clearing his throat. "Unless someone else wants to do it, guess I will. Let's bow our heads. Father, thanks for gettin' us here safe. Father, thanks for the food we ate. Father, thanks for our friends and family. Father, keep us safe here. Father, in Jesus' name. Amen."

He unfurled his piece of paper and smoothed it slowly with his hands. "Um, tonight I thought I'd tell ya about how Moses led God's people into the Promised Land."

Never mind that Paw didn't seem to realize Moses never actually made it into the Promised Land. I was proud to see my father reading to us from the Bible. Mom had told me that Paw had a heart that loved Jesus, but this was the first time I'd seen him really talk about it beyond an occasional prayer or a warning to us kids about obeying God. After Paw finished reading to us from the book of

Exodus, his expression turned stern.

"Now, if we want to keep God happy with us, there are some rules we need to follow. Number one. No cussin'. That means you, too, Bantom. We got kids here."

Mr. Bantom chuckled. "I'll try to keep it clean."

"Number two. Everyone needs to be here on time for the meetin' each night. Number three. No drinkin'. Alcohol, that is. Sorry, again, Bantom, but we can't have no drunken brawls around here. God wouldn't like that. Number four. If it ain't legal back in town, it ain't legal here neither. That goes for everything. We need to respect each other's things, too. And if you can't work out a problem, come to me. That is, unless your gripe's with me." Everyone laughed. "Guess that's about all I have unless anybody's got questions."

I raised my hand.

"Yes, Lulu. I mean, Effie."

"I was wonderin' why the Derryhills have so many—" Mom put her hand over my mouth and Paw quickly dismissed us.

"Now go put your kids to bed. That goes double for mine. You can wash up out front. We've put a big ole pan of water out there to sponge off with. And kids, don't forget to take a flashlight out of that box over yonder to keep with you at night. Even when you're in bed."

The other folks left the cabin. Mom walked to where Paw stood and wrapped her arms around him. She leaned her head back and looked into his eyes.

"You did it! See there was nothing to be afraid of. You did great!"

"Good job, Paw. Only, Moses didn't really—" Mom stopped me before I gave him my Bible lesson. She whispered to me later not to burst his bubble, or something like that.

The steady cadence of Roy Boy's breathing assured me he was sound asleep enough to make my escape. With flashlight in hand, I slipped out through the open front door and tiptoed my way to the tent where the grown-ups were meeting.

A distorted play of silhouetted figures took place in front of me on the side of the tarp. I had to hold my laughter as Paw rose to speak. His shadow appeared to be ten feet tall as he lifted his arms to make a point.

"In about a week's time," I heard him say, "they'll be lookin' for us and wonderin' what the heck happened to us. We need to be ready and watchful of our borders."

Our borders? Looking for us? I didn't understand.

"The President's callin' for gas rationin' to start just any day now, and when it does, all heck's gonna break out. They'll declare martial law, and you know what that means!"

Shadowy heads nodded their agreement and a woman let out a loud sigh. Deciding I'd heard enough, I daintily trotted back to my cabin and stopped cold on the doorstep. Covering my face to protect against spider webs, I dashed to my cot, pulled the covers over my head and wished for the morning sun.

CHAPTER SIX

The next ten days flew by, filled with activity. Paw led the troops, barking orders like a drill sergeant to his young recruits. We had beautiful, yet humid, weather so Paw often remarked, "We need to make hay while the sun shines." I hoped for a day of showers. *When are we going to play all those games Mom talked about?*

Roy Boy, Timmy and I were put in charge of gathering rocks and stacking them behind our cabin.

"We'll find a lot of use for these," Paw said, digging a large, half-buried stone out of the ground. He handed it to me and motioned toward the pile that nearly rose to my waist.

"Cain't have all these rocks in our garden." Paw took a noisy gulp from his canteen and wiped his forehead with the back of his grimy arm. "Pray for some rain to soften the ground for us," he muttered. With a shovel in his hand, he walked back across the property to where the other men were digging a trench leading from the designated garden spot to the broad creek. This would be our irrigation system,

Paw told me.

I watched as they rhythmically shoveled dirt. I couldn't understand why they weren't working to finish the walls for those living in the tent-cabins. My attention was mostly on Mr. Chris as he slaved in the heat, peeling off layers until he was wearing only his cut-off shorts and hiking boots. Poor Mr. Chris. His legs and arms were covered with bug bites, but he didn't complain.

The trench was slowly getting longer and longer. As they dug, the men cast rocks onto the ground on either side of the hole. I rolled the wheelbarrow over to the trench and gathered what the older men had unearthed. I then made my way to the stack behind Mr. Chris, and began carrying the stones to the waiting wheelbarrow, one in each hand.

"Anyone need water yet?" I said, as I picked up the last two.

"I could use some. If you don't mind." Mr. Chris said to me, shading his face from the bright afternoon sun.

I grabbed the wheelbarrow and wobbled a few feet before tipping my load. I hurriedly gathered the rocks I dumped and continued to the "base" pile. I took them out as quickly as I could — I had a thirsty man waiting — and placed each rock on the top of the pile. My goal was to create a mountain as high as my shoulders if I could ever keep the rocks from tumbling down the side of the stack.

I wiped my hands on my shorts, poured the cup of water and carefully walked back, not wanting to spill a drop.

Mr. Chris drank the water down and wiped the dribble from his chin, leaving a tawny streak of mud across his face.

"Thanks!" I said, taking the empty cup from him. I was

awestruck over the thought that this very cup had been held in his hands and lifted to his lips.

"No. Thank YOU. That was sweet of you."

I wasn't aware I was staring at him until Paw said, "Got an admirer there."

The men chuckled as I ran away in embarrassment only to arrive back to the picnic area to see my brother snickering and punching Timmy on the arm. I could tell by the expression on Timmy's face he must've heard Paw and was having a difficult time holding back his own laughter.

"Effie's got a boyfriend! Effie's got a boyfriend!" Roy Boy jeered.

"Teliot ecaf," I said, leaning into Roy Boy close enough to give him a full-fingernailed pinch on his arm. "EEEEyor!" I said, digging my nails even further into his tortured arm. He wailed like a banshee.

"You little—" he eeked out.

I shot him a threatening, squinty-eyed look and noticed that Timmy backed up a few steps and put his arms behind his back.

"I'm taking a break for a while and goin' on a walk." I knew no one would protest, nor dare tell on me. I'd taken care of that situation just fine. Mom was inside the cabin with Mrs. Derryhill and Michelle, preparing the peanut butter sandwiches for lunch. Peanut butter had become our every-other-day lunch.

After glancing around quickly to make sure I wasn't spotted, I darted to the camp's exit and scurried through the brush that concealed the path down the hill. Tippy came along, keeping a couple of feet ahead of me the entire time. I knew the way because Mom and I took that path looking for edible herbs in the woods. I'd been warned never to go without an adult. *Does Tippy count as an adult? He's 63 in dog years.* The feeling in my gut told me I had probably crossed over into the area of doing something wrong. Mom had told me over and over that if something isn't right, then it's wrong. Ignoring the feeling, I continued my descent, pushing small branches out of the way.

There it was dead ahead. The marrying tree stood just to the left of the path. Its leaves were full and plentiful now, its shade inviting. I reached my hand into my pocket and grasped the pocketknife I'd swiped out of Roy Boy's gear earlier in the day. Another wrong I'd committed. Taking a deep breath, I pried open the blade and approached the tree. Taking note of the suspicious vine wrapped around its trunk and thinking I'd better keep this covert, I decided it best to move to the back of the tree, facing away from the path. I put the blade to the crusty bark and began to chisel. This proved to be more difficult than I thought it would be. The bark was tough and unyielding beneath my strokes, so I pushed harder until pieces began to chip away: "EW + C" — *what was his last name? Monroe? Montgomery? Have I even heard his last name?* I carved an "M" after the "C" because I was fairly certain his name started with that. Besides, I knew who I was talking about, so that was all that mattered.

"Marrying Tree?" I whispered. "I love Mr. Chris. Don't tell anyone. It's our secret. So now that I've told you, I guess he'll ask me to marry him someday? Sorry about cutting you with the knife. I won't do it anymore." I hugged the tree, avoiding the vine, of course, and ran my fingers across the freshly-cut initials. The fragrance on my fingertips was crisp and sharp, the way my hands smell when I've pulled weeds in the yard.

"Come on, Tippy!"

He ran alongside as I hiked up the hill past the Virginia-Creeper-covered trees. *Or is that poison ivy?* I arrived back to the brush at the camp entrance just in time to hear Mom calling out to the men that lunch was ready. I waited until she turned around toward the cabin before emerging and entering the clearing. Tippy was already at the picnic area begging for a hand-out by the time I reached it.

"Go wash up," Mom told the kids. "And make sure you get all the dirt out from under your nails. You don't want worms."

Worms? Can I really get worms? I scratched my arms and then looked under my nails for any sign of the wiggling things. I scrubbed like never before. I felt around for Roy Boy's knife, but my pockets were empty. It was gone. Now worms seemed good to me compared to the consequences I'd face once he discovered it missing. I scratched a little bit more and began to plot my strategy for finding the knife. My wrong act was about to get "wronger."

CHAPTER SEVEN

A midnight rainstorm startled me awake with a terrifying flash and crack which caused me to yank the covers far over my eyes in a knee-jerk reaction. This event repeated itself several times over the next two hours. Now I understand what people mean when they say they had a restless night. Unable to return to my slumber, my mind immediately returned to the thought that occupied my brain throughout my bedtime prayer — *Where is Roy Boy's knife, and how will I get it back?*

The clouds wrung their last drops just as the sky glowed faintly beyond the camp's tree-lined border. The adults had stayed up late last night making plans as they played bridge, so I knew Mom and Paw would remain in bed later than usual. This was my only chance.

I slowly rose, making only one "boing" as the cot's metallic springs shifted under my weight. Roy Boy didn't stir. Only Tippy looked up and seemed mildly curious about my early rising. I slid my feet into my slippers and crept my way toward the cabin door. Realizing I forgot my flashlight,

I took Roy Boy's from beside his cot. He wouldn't need it. The sun was almost up.

Tippy jingled as he sauntered behind me. Amazingly, Roy Boy didn't move a muscle and even looked fairly angelic as he lay curled in a fetal position. I felt a twinge of guilt about swiping his knife, *and now I've snatched his flashlight.*

With my face covered, I walked across the short front porch, jumping when a cobweb brushed the back of my hand. Deep, red clay puddles surrounded the porch. I had to stretch my leg out far to set my foot down on solid ground before letting go of the porch rail. Tippy leapt from the porch effortlessly and ran ahead to do his business. This triggered my own urge to visit the outhouse, but there was no time to waste. The sun was peeking through the dense hardwoods on the horizon, and Mom and Paw would soon be awake and notice I was missing.

I continued carrying out the plan I'd concocted the night before of revisiting the last place I remember seeing the pocketknife—the marrying tree. So, dodging puddles, I took the familiar path down the hill, past the dripping trees and glistening spider-web-covered undergrowth. Tippy acted strangely, and I couldn't shake the feeling we were not alone on that path. In the distance, down the hill, I saw the back of a man standing near the marrying tree. I stopped walking, preparing to run, but not before the man turned around to face me.

Knock smiled. A wave of relief ran over my body, and my knees buckled slightly before straightening.

"You scared the devil outta me, Knock!"

I walked to him and wanted to give him a hug, which I

would've done if we hadn't met under such lonely circumstances.

"I didn't know you were here. Where are you living?"

Knock smoothed back his flaxen hair.

"Nearby," was his reply. "I'm not too far away."

"Why don't you come back to camp with me and say 'hi' to Paw? He'll be excited to have a guest."

"In due time. I'll let you get settled first."

"Did you happen to see a pocketknife sittin' around anywhere? I lost one and will get killed if Roy Boy finds out it's gone."

"This it?" Knock said, holding the knife out to me.

"Gee, thanks! You saved my hide! I'd better get back before anyone knows I'm down here. I ain't supposed to wander off by myself."

"Then you'd best be gone. You should always mind your parents. They love you very much and want you to be safe." Knock winked and turned away.

I ran halfway up the hill, then turned to see in which direction Knock walked, but he had already gone from my sight. I was pleased to know I had a friend living nearby, although my family said he didn't exist.

When I arrived back to the cabin, Roy Boy was awake but still lying in bed.

"Where've you been?" he asked, wiping the drool from his mouth.

"Potty."

"How come you're covered with them sticker things. There ain't no bushes between here and the outhouse."

"I looked to see if there were any blackberries yet on the bushes over that way," I said, gesturing toward the right.

"You're crazy. Go back to sleep and quit roaming around. Mom and Paw will get mad at you if they find out."

"Pord daed."

"Drop dead, yourself, and stop that stupid backwards-talkin' It's annoying."

"Why do you think I do it, Eyor?" I said, bending over to stick my tongue out at him as I slid the flashlight and pocketknife under his cot.

I was so proud to have carried off the act without creating suspicion. Roy Boy would, hopefully, remain ignorant as to my whereabouts earlier. With his personal articles placed under his cot, I could convince him that I heard a clunk in the middle of the night, hence his flashlight falling out of bed. The pocketknife might be a little more difficult to explain, but with a little craftiness, I should be able to slip it back into his pack.

Mom ambled out of her bedroom door, wrapping a bathrobe tightly around her voluminous body.

"What's all the commotion out here? Effie, why aren't you in bed?"

My worst nightmare. Roy Boy was lying in bed watching me as I struggled for the words, so I had to tell the same lie to Mom. My gut wrenched as the words spilled out.

"Potty and berry huntin'. I wanted to surprise you with some blackberries for breakfast." I was getting remarkably good at ad-libbing, well, actually lying, but I somehow didn't feel too proud of myself over this new-found talent.

"That's sweet of you, but you know the berries won't be ripe for a while yet. I don't want you out wanderin' around by yourself. I've told you that. Especially when everyone's in bed. Why don't I fix you some oatmeal since you're up?"

Paw came out of the room, rubbing his scruffy face with both hands.

"Pretty early for you to be up, Lulu. Something wrong?" He walked to the coffee kettle and touched it quickly to see if it was hot. Mom was starting a fire in the stone fireplace, which I knew would soon make the cabin unbearably hot.

"The generator should be fixed any time now," Paw said. "Bantom's gonna sneak into town and get us a part from the garage. Then we'll be able to use that old stove. You'll just have to bear with the heat a couple more days, or use the fire pit for cookin.' Lulu? You didn't answer me. Is something the matter? Why'd you go out wanderin' by yourself?"

"Nothing's the matter," I said. Roy Boy didn't seem to be buying my story completely as he peeked at me from under his covers.

"Besides. I wasn't really by myself. Knock was with me." I knew the instant those words came out of my mouth I should not have spoken them.

"Knock?" Paw said, looking at Mom. "Where'd you see 'im?"

"He was just outside. By some trees."

Paw looked troubled, which I thought was a strange reaction to have over my "make-believe" friend. I had forgotten that Mom didn't want me mentioning him in front of Paw after my meeting with the doctor.

"Why, isn't it nice for you to have a friend around," Mom commented, sounding like she was trying to make light of the situation. "But, Effie. I don't think he qualifies as having someone around. You know that."

Paw remained quiet as Mom placed the coffee pot on the rack above the fire. She perched on a stool until steam rose from the top of the kettle. As she poured the hot water through a coffee-filled filter, it dribbled out black and fragrant.

"He lives nearby." *Why did I say that?*

"Nearby where?" Paw asked, peering from under his furrowed brow.

"I dunno. He didn't tell me where exactly. Just nearby."

Mom slowly stirred the iron pot of oatmeal. She looked back at me and mouthed "be quiet", before glancing back at Paw, smiling.

I studied the worried look on Paw's face. *Maybe I should remind him about my anxiety? The doctor said I had too many changes in my life. Or maybe I should keep my big mouth shut.*

That evening after devotion time, a special meeting was called for the adults. I surmised there was something on Pa's mind because he cut the Bible reading short and ignored me when I raised my hand and asked if we could sing "Jesus Loves Me."

After Mom tucked me and Roy Boy in bed, Paw came in the room and told us goodnight before heading to Mr. Bantom's tent-cabin, where the special meeting was to be held. Even though I had not slept much the night before, curiosity won out over my exhaustion. I had to know what was so important. Roy Boy seemed intent on staying awake that night, and I was afraid I'd miss the meeting if I waited for him to nod off, so I invited him to come along. I was pleasantly surprised that he wanted to join me. Now he wouldn't be able to tell on me without incriminating himself, too.

We put our sneakers on and crept to Mr. Bantom's place, positioning ourselves on the side where we could see the shadows. Roy Boy giggled as we watched. I threw my hand over his mouth and jabbed him in the side with my other elbow. "Shhh."

Paw told the group my history of anxiety and how I'd mentioned seeing my imaginary friend, Knock, earlier in the day. I was embarrassed to think that Mr. Chris would find me childish and silly. I wished I could tell him the truth – that Knock was real, and I only played along with my parents to appease them.

"Ahh, Whatley. You can't mean that Effie's make-believe friend is a threat, can you?" I heard Mr. Derryhill ask.

"What I mean," Paw said in a serious tone, "is that we cain't take no chances around here. No one can know where we are or there'll be trouble."

Mr. Chris let out a mumbled "give me a break" and shuffled in his seat. His shadow was straight in front of where I sat.

"Chris, I'm serious about this. I don't need for anyone to take this lightly. The government is real close to declaring martial law and when that happens, all heck'll break loose. They won't let no one have no gasoline, 'cept their small ration, then no one will be able to work. If no one works, there won't be no eatin'. If there ain't nothing to eat, then there'll be a lot of stealin'. People'll be taking anything they can get their hands on. Especially guns, gasoline and food. After all, that's why we're here. To protect ourselves from the government's intrusion. It's our God-given right to have our guns and gas, so we're gonna make sure they don't take our rights away from us." Paw sounded heated.

"How are we going to do that?" Michelle asked.

I saw Paw's shadowy figure hold up a rifle and cock it. A couple of ladies gasped.

"It's for our protection, ladies," Paw said softly.

"Seems drastic to me," Mrs. Derryhill replied.

"Not drastic if someone's coming after you to take your liberties away."

"Who exactly would come all the way out here to do that?" Mr. Chris asked.

Paw laughed. "The government officials cain't wait to run our lives. They'll have the National Guard out. You name it. They'll be lookin' for anyone who has supplies they want. You know that gasoline we got stored in them barrels out there? People would be willin' to kill for gas once they're told they can't have it anymore. We only need enough to run our generator and to put in our car if we need to go into town for anything. Gotta make sure we have enough to get back when all of this is over and we can go home."

"How long will that be?" Michelle asked.

"Long as it takes, Michelle. In the meantime, Bantom and me will protect the camp against intruders best we can. We're both armed and will keep a lookout. I know Effie's friend is make-believe, but we can't take no chances. If you see a man hangin' around, let me know and I'll take care of it. He can stay with us, but I guarantee he won't go back to give away our location."

I trembled and scratched until I felt moisture on my forearm. I lifted my fingers to my nose and smelled the familiar metallic scent of blood.

"Let's go back," I whispered to Roy Boy. "I've heard enough."

He picked up his flashlight and turned it on as soon as we stepped away from the tent-cabin. Paw may be determined to protect the camp, but my new priority was to protect Knock.

CHAPTER EIGHT

———•●•———

"What's this one?" I asked Mom, pointing to the jar full of dried leaves.

"Chamomile. Remember the tea I made for you when you had a hard time falling asleep? That's what it was made from."

I removed the lid from the jar and drew in a deep breath. "Ooo. I like that." I began removing the lids from each one, rating them from one to fifteen. Mom told me the name and use of each herb after my score.

"Spearmint's my very favorite. Peppermint is second. And lavender comes in third," I said, gently replacing each lid and pretending to stick a ribbon on the front just like I'd seen judges do at the county fair.

"Now, let me see if I can remember what they are. I scrambled the jars around and set them on the shelves Paw built. I knew Mom would have no problem getting them back in order. She'd dried many of the herbs herself before we came to the camp. The others were acquired from a lady in town who taught Mom how to forage.

"Comfrey. Nettles. Rosemary. Jewelweed. Calendula – yum – my number four favorite. Sorry, but I don't have a ribbon for you," I said, patting the top of the jar. "Maybe you'll taste better than one of the others and earn a ribbon, too." I went down the long row of jars, identifying each one and only stumbling on tansy and feverfew.

"Very impressive. But can you name them with your eyes closed?" Mom asked.

I closed my eyes, and mom rearranged the jars. She opened each lid and held the jar under my nose. When I was finished naming them, she pretended to place a ribbon around my neck.

"Best nose in the camp," she said, patting me on the head. "You really are amazing." She shook her head, smiling, as she turned back and resumed chopping nuts on the kitchen table. "I'll have to take you foraging again and show you where some more of these grow. Maybe we can even add a few things to our supply."

"Mom? What does that mean?" I said, tapping the front of one jar.

"That's called a skull and crossbones. It means you'd best not make tea with the herbs in those jars." Mom pointed to three jars bearing the same symbol. "They could give you a tummy ache. They're for the outside of your body, not the inside."

"So that's supposed to be a dead guy?"

"I reckon," Mom replied. "Go tell your Paw that breakfast is ready."

"Can I have some tea with my breakfast?"

"May I. And yes, you may."

Mom dipped the little silver ball into the hot water, and

I watched as bubbles escaped from each hole. I waved my hand over the steam and sniffed the air.

"Spearmint!"

"Yes, indeed. Gotta have your first place winner."

"Tomorrow, maybe I can have number two, then number three the next day. But I won't drink any with the bonehead guy on front."

Mom set the hot mug in front of me. I dipped a small amount out and slurped it off the spoon. Paw and Roy Boy took their places at the table across from me and Mom.

"Yuk! That's awful."

Mom laughed and placed the sugar bowl next to my mug.

"Just 'cause it smells good don't mean it tastes good!" Paw snickered and sipped his coffee. "Never was one to like all that tea stuff myself."

"Me either." Roy Boy added. "That's for girls."

"You'll like it if you start feeling poorly one day! Nothing like a warm cup of herbal tea to soothe a sour stomach," Mom said, winking at me. "See if you don't like it better now that you've sweetened it up."

"Yum. Now it tastes good! Paw don't know what's he's missing."

"Yeah, I do. Bleh. But I admit. It does smell good. Sorta like candy."

My thoughts suddenly switched to what I'd heard Paw say in the tent the night before, and I hesitated before opening my mouth to ask him the question on my mind.

"Paw? Would you ever hurt Knock if you saw him?"

"Why would I want to hurt someone who's make-believe?" He cleared his throat two times, then scooped his runny eggs onto a piece of toast. "He is make-believe. Right?"

"Sure is. The doctor even said so. Doctors are real smart, so we have to believe what they say. There's no point in being afraid of a make-believe guy."

"Why do you ask, Lulu?" Paw glanced at Mom, who raised her eyebrows at me.

"No reason, really. Just wondered. He wouldn't hurt a fly . . . I mean, if he was real."

Mom abruptly changed the subject. "Effie, hurry up and finish your breakfast so we can go pick some greens and herbs. It'll be fun, don't you think?"

"'Spose so. Why do we need more anyway?"

"I thought it might be a good learning experience for you."

"But it's summer break, so I don't need to be learning right now," I answered.

"You'll be learning all your life, Honey. That never ends. Besides, what else do you have planned?" She grinned and looked at Paw.

"Paw still needs me to gather rocks. Right?"

"You go do like your Mom tells you. We've just about finished our trench, so there ain't much else for you to do," Paw said, wiping his mouth with the napkin that was tucked in the front of his shirt.

"Roy Boy needs to be learning, too." I shifted my gaze to my older brother, who rolled his eyes at my remark. "If I have to learn, he does, too."

"Lulu, Roy Boy's gonna be helping with the men today. He'll be learnin' plenty, so don't you worry about that." Paw chuckled and shook his head. "You're something else. Mr. Chris will still be around for you to visit with.”

I was horrified to think that he may have said something to Mr. Chris.

“I don’t like Mr. Chris,” I mumbled under my breath. My face burned and showed me to be lying.

“Why’d you have to say that to her? Now she’s embarrassed.” Mom reached over and smoothed back a piece of hair from my face. “I think Mr. Chris is a fine young man. I would’ve liked him, too, if I wasn’t married. Now run along and get your shoes on.”

Mom and I started our search at the edge of the creek.

“Now study your surroundings for a moment,” she said, breathing in the fresh air.

I looked closely at the vegetation, never before noticing how many different-looking plants existed. The sight was a bit strange to me — pointy plants, tiny plants, bushy, dark green, light green plants — all growing out of a patch of dirt no longer my out-stretched arms.

“Which picture do you think this one looks like,” she said, pointing to one plant growing out of the creek’s bank. I looked at the page Mom had opened in her field guide and studied the five photos. Each was similar to the next, so it was difficult for me to tell the difference.

“Maybe this one?”

“Why did you choose that one?” Mom asked.

“Because it has that thing there. Looks like a little curly cue.”

“All ferns have those when the new shoots are opening, but guess what?”

“What?”

“You’re right! You chose the correct photo. You’ll

make a great forager!"

"Are you gonna pull that up and eat it, Mom?"

"No. I'm not gonna eat a fern. I came out here to look for plants we can use in our salad."

By the end of the afternoon, Mom had filled her basket with a variety of greens. I wondered what they would taste like and couldn't imagine eating anything that had been pulled up from the ground. It all looked like things I'd seen growing in the yard back home. Although I'd chewed on a piece of grass from time to time, the thought of swallowing it didn't sound appealing to me in the least.

Mom washed our harvest and put it into a large bowl. She fluffed the leaves which had become a little matted from the washing and set the salad next to a large serving fork on the picnic table.

"I know it doesn't look like much," she told the campers, now assembled for dinner. "Effie and I gathered this today, so it's nice and fresh. I want everyone to take some salad and eat it because these greens are a good source of vitamins. There's enough for each to take about this much," Mom said, showing her plate which held several leaves.

The Derryhills looked frightened. Timmy whispered something to his mother, who shook her head in reply.

"I'm not gonna be shy! I'm hungry!" Chris plopped a hot dog on his plate and speared several leaves with a fork. He pushed them off the fork with his fingers and examined them closely. "How'd you know you could eat this, Effie? That's real impressive."

I thought I would die! Mr. Chris had complimented my intelligence and now was going to eat something I gathered for him!

When all the plates were served, I looked around to see how well the salad had been received. I noticed the Derryhills had each taken one leaf and had not touched them. Mike and Michelle nibbled delicately and nodded their approval to each other.

"I feel like a goat grazin' on grass," Paw said as he chewed a piece of chickweed. "Cain't say as I like it too much, but I'm thankful the good Lord gave it to us to eat."

"Yuk! It's like chewing on the front yard at home," Roy Boy said.

"How do you know what the front yard tastes like, Eyor? Watch out for the poison ivy on your plate," I whispered to him.

"You wouldn't have done that, 'cause Mr. Chris woulda—"

I threw my hand over his mouth to cover it before he could continue.

"Mom. Roy Boy is sayin' bad things about our salad."

"You both need to be quiet and eat," she replied.

I chewed some greens and turned my head toward Roy Boy, opening my mouth long enough for him to see. I knew he hated the sight of chewed food. On a good day, I could make him gag. Truthfully, I wanted to spit those bitter greens out of my mouth and onto my plate, but I swallowed and held my breath until the taste had subsided a little. When the last bite of salad was gone from my plate, I faked a smile and wiped my mouth.

"Refreshing!" I said, after swallowing a gulp of water. "Can I go out and play?"

"May I," Mom corrected.

"You can play 'bout fifteen minutes," Paw said, looking at his watch. "But don't be late for devotion time."

"I won't!" I scurried off with Tippy at my side. *I wonder where Knock lives?* I scanned the perimeter of the camp, then decided I had enough time to search over by the creek before evening came.

— • ● • —

I tip-toed toward my cabin where the group was meeting. Through the open doorway, I could see Paw standing, addressing the folks, cutting his eyes in my direction. *Uh, oh.* This was the first time I'd been late for devotions, and by the look on Paw's face, it had better be the last.

"Glad you could join us, Effie." It was not a good sign that Paw called me by my given name. That meant certain consequences later.

"We're talking about right and wrong, Effie. We have the Ten Commandments to tell us what we should and shouldn't do. Who can tell us what they are? Anyone remember?" Paw looked around and started the list off. "Don't kill and steal," he said, holding up two fingers.

"Don't work on Sunday!" Roy Boy shouted.

Paw asked, "Effie, is there one about minding you might could tell us?"

"Um. Let me see . . . ." I strained to remember what I'd learned in Sunday school back home. "Honor your father and your mother?"

"That's right. When your Paw tells you to be at devotion time and you show up fifteen minutes late, that's not honorin'. 'Fraid I'll need to see you after the meeting."

I really wished Paw hadn't said that in front of everyone. Especially Mr. Chris.

Paw continued, "Now, where were we? Oh, yeah. We were naming the commandments."

"No lying. No adultery. And no saying things like 'Oh, God' or 'Oh, Lord'," Michelle said, looking toward us kids.

Timmy lowered his head slightly and softly said, "Don't worship idols." His mother beamed at him.

Have I ever heard Timmy say anything in front of a bunch of people?

Mom cleared her throat and said, "Don't wish for something that belongs to your neighbor."

I'd always heard the word 'covet' used but didn't realize it meant 'want'. I supposed I'd broken two commandments today. Just this morning I thought about my neighbor's pretty red bicycle and wished I had it here to ride around camp.

"What did Jesus say was the greatest commandment?" Paw asked. "He said to love God with all your heart and soul and mind."

I thought it was not to kill, with not stealing a close second.

Paw tapped his chin two times with a pointed finger, before raising it toward heaven, wagging it back and forth. I wondered what point he was getting ready to make and hoped it didn't involve my transgressions.

"How can we show God how much we love Him? By doing what's right. If I've said it once, I've said it a thousand times to my kids. If it ain't right, then it's wrong. There ain't no 'sorta right' or 'sorta wrong'. You're either right or you're wrong. Period."

"Yep. He says that all the time!" I spoke out. "You also say 'spare the rod and spoil the child'. That's from the Bible, too. You say that all the time before you spank us." *Why did I say that?*

The group laughed. They seemed to know a spanking was waiting for me because I was late to devotions.

There ought to be a commandment against laughing at kids when they're in trouble.

Mr. Chris cocked his head sympathetically and pouted his lips as he looked my way. *At least he feels sorry for me.*

Paw asked for someone to close in prayer, but before anyone volunteered, Michelle stood.

"I just want to thank everyone for being so nice to me and Mike. We didn't know you well before we came here, but now you're family. Thanks, too, for going to the trouble of finding nutritious stuff for us to eat from the woods. My baby thanks you, too." She rubbed her belly and looked around at each face. "We found out before the planning meeting back home but didn't want to tell anyone yet. We wanted to see if I felt well enough to continue with the plans."

The grown-ups looked stunned. Especially Paw, whose mouth hung wide open. After a moment, Mom and Mrs. Derryhill rose and hugged Michelle.

Mom grabbed Michelle's hand and said, "We'll help you out all we can. That's exciting news!"

Mrs. Derryhill nodded. "Indeed. My Timmy is the joy of my life!"

I noticed the tense stare between Paw and Mr. Bantom. They looked as if they knew something the rest of us didn't.

"Bantom. Can I see you for a moment when we're finished here?" Mr. Bantom nodded at Paw.

Maybe Michelle just saved my hide.

CHAPTER NINE

— • ● • —

"**Vinca. We cain't** have no baby in the camp!" Paw pounded his fist on the kitchen table, his jaw set and teeth clenched.

"But it won't be any trouble, Pomeroy," Mom said. "There'll be three grown women helping Michelle and the baby. You men won't be bothered at all."

"What's she gonna do? Give birth on a cot? You need a clean place for something like that. And you need doctors and a hospital. I can fix cars, but I cain't fix people if something goes wrong."

"I can read up on being a midwife. I have a book with a chapter on that. I'm sure we can handle it. You used to help your uncle birth calves on his farm. It isn't that different," Mom said.

"There ain't no 'we' about it. I'm not helping deliver a human baby. That's Mike's job," Paw said, pointing toward the door. "There's nothin' we can do about it now. The baby will be here before you know it, crying all the time. Someone's bound to find us with all that racket going on.

What's done is done, I suppose," Paw said, crossing his arms tightly.

"What do you expect a young couple to do? Wait until the crisis is over before starting a family? Who knows how long that will be?" Mom asked. She smoothed my hair and continued, "They just want their baby to be safe. We came here to keep our kids safe, so you can't blame them for doing the same thing."

Paw looked at me and Roy Boy. "I suppose you're right, but it just seems like the responsible thing woulda been to tell us they're expectin' before following us up here."

"I think you're worrying about nothing. No one will hear the baby cry." Mom reassured. "Except us." She chuckled. "There's not a soul around for miles. Besides, we may be back home before the baby is born."

Paw let out a long sigh and rubbed his brow. "We'll make sure their cabin is finished first. They'll need their privacy. And we'll make it as airtight as possible 'cause I don't wanna hear no baby squawlin'."

"Now you're talking like the kind man I married." Mom kissed Paw on the cheek and walked to the cots to turn down the covers. "Time to go to sleep, kids."

Mom sat on Roy Boy's cot first, then mine, listening to our prayers and kissing us on the forehead.

From my bed, I heard them banter back and forth for the next hour. Obviously, Paw still wasn't 100% convinced that having a baby around was a good idea. *All this fuss about a baby who won't even be born for a long time.* I couldn't understand why Paw was so upset about it. *It's just a cute little baby.* Paw kept bringing up Mr. Bantom's name and how angry he was about the news of a baby in Michelle's tummy. *Simple. Michelle can have her baby in the hospital when we get back. What's all the fuss about?*

— • ● • —

The men busied themselves completing the other cabins. The sound of hammering was non-stop the entire time the sun was up, and I could see that Mike and Michelle's cabin was finished except for the windows. In the evenings, I noticed the air becoming a little cooler and wondered how long it would be until school started back. *Why are they bothering to get the cabins built when we all have houses we'll go back to soon?* They spent days and days constructing fireplaces, which seemed like a waste of time to me since we wouldn't be at the camp in the winter.

"You won't be going back to school this year, Effie," was Mom's answer when I asked her about it. I didn't know how to reply, and I sensed it was best not to ask why. I also noticed a growing tension in Paw. The evening meetings grew longer and longer, so I knew there were serious things happening they were keeping from telling us kids.

I wanted to go home, but that wasn't in the plans, so when my fear of the unknown became overwhelming, I'd find solace in the surrounding woods. The trees were strong and stable; their shelter was soothing.

My foraging skills were improving, but many of the plants Mom and I had been collecting all summer were beginning to fade away. She said there would be new things to look for — things that would survive the cold weather. Cold weather. Those words frightened me. I had to hold onto my hope that we'd be back in Burnt Willow before cold weather arrived.

A few summer plants remained in our garden, though the cool summer evenings caused their fruit to be less than stellar. We tilled the rest of the soil with shovels and hoes getting it ready for our fall crop to be planted.

Mr. Bantom knew a man back in town who raised chickens.

"Go see him, Roy. He can keep a secret," I heard Mr. Bantom tell Paw one night. "He wouldn't mind gettin' us some hens."

Paw sneaked into town one evening and purchased a few layers. He said that was the last time he would risk being found out, as things were "heating up." He couldn't take any more chances at being seen. The fresh eggs were a wonderful change, and I felt worth the risk.

I loved the hens and would climb into their pen to look for eggs each morning. Tippy wasn't permitted to get near them for fear he would enjoy a nice chicken dinner. *Poor Tippy*. He spent a great deal of the day tied to a porch post to keep him from wandering toward the chicken pen. Paw allowed him to be let off the rope if Roy Boy and I, together, accompanied him wherever he went. Tippy favored the creek and would sit on the bank watching me and Roy Boy throw pebbles into the deep pool downstream.

Like the rolling water swishing over the smooth river rocks, our lives had settled into a comfortable and predictable rhythm. We gathered, watered plants, and baked in the mornings. Cleaning was done on Tuesdays. Foraging on Wednesdays. Washing clothes at the creek on Thursdays, and so on. After doing our chores, we kids worked on school lessons Mom had prepared for us, then spent our early afternoons playing. We would untie Tippy and head to the creek to go wading or fishing, often taking the long way back in order to climb a tree or two. We played hide and seek on clear days, and Old Maid or Charades inside the cabin when the weather was stormy. During the daylight hours, I didn't mind the rain. I found the pinging of drops on the tin roof to be cozy, especially with Tippy curled next to me.

In the evenings, Roy Boy, Timmy, and I would catch fireflies and throw small stones into the air to watch the bats dive for them. After eating dinner together, there would be devotion time, followed by an "adults only" meeting where they would discuss plans for the coming day. I don't know why they needed to plan anything, because our schedule varied only a little from day to day. Mom told me that adults just need time to be adults and talk about things that matter to them.

As time went on, I grew to enjoy life here; it was peaceful and good. Although our routine was consistent, we never got bored. There were no regrets, and I never thought about what I might be missing back home during those days. This had become home for me.

We spent more time with Paw than we ever had before. I was proud of him and the way people looked up to him at the camp. I think Mom was proud, too. I heard her make the comment to Mrs. Derryhill about how Paw had really come out of his shell, and how she would have never imagined how much he'd enjoy a leadership position. He had always been a soft-spoken, behind-the-scenes kind of man. I don't know if she ever told Paw these things to his face, but their relationship had taken on a contentment I'd never seen back in Burnt Willow.

"This is the way kids should be brought up," Paw would often remark as he sat at the picnic table. I believe he felt good about making this lifestyle possible for us.

After dinner each evening, Paw would walk up behind Mom and rub her tired, rounded shoulders. His small slender fingers seemed dwarfed by Mom's bulky back. As he kneaded, he'd move Mom's long hair off to one side, then the other. Paw never seemed to tire of this.

"That feels so good," she'd purr, and reach up to pat his hands as a signal that her tired muscles were now okay, and he could rest.

"Are you happy here?" he would ask her with predictable frequency.

"Very," was always her response.

The only person who looked as if he didn't share that sentiment was Mr. Chris. He had become more and more distant in recent days. I wondered if he felt left out. Mike had been a close friend of his for several years before coming to the camp. Now Michelle was expecting a baby, so Mike's attention seemed to be completely on her. Mike had gone from a touch football-playing young man, to a "homebody", as Mom called him.

"He'll make a great dad," she commented, watching him read to his wife after dinner one evening. Her feet were propped in a chair, her head rested on a bundled jacket.

"As good as Paw?" I asked her.

"That remains to be seen," she answered.

"Mom, when are we going back to Burnt Willow?"

"Why do you ask? Do you want to leave?" she asked.

I shrugged. "I don't know."

Mom turned her head to face me. "Don't you like it here?"

"Yeah. I like it. Just wondered."

"We'll be here a while, Honey. Until we're sure it's okay to go back," she said.

"The gas thing? And that martial law stuff Paw talks about?"

Mom smiled. "That's right."

"Paw said that things would get ugly. Has it gotten ugly yet, Mom?"

"I really don't know, Effie. But don't worry about it. It won't affect us up here." She reached over and pulled my scratching fingers away from my arm.

"Then I want to stay here, Mom." I looked at the trees surrounding the camp. "I feel safe here."

Mom smiled and patted my leg. "I'm glad."

———•●•———

I'm not sure what caused me to wake. Probably the voices I heard on the porch. I got out of bed and crept to the front door to see what was going on. Upon reaching the open door, I heard Mom speaking softly to a man.

"She's cramping and asked me to get you." I recognized the voice as belonging to Mike.

"Let me get dressed, and I'll be right over." Mom came

inside and startled at the sight of me standing in her flashlight's beam.

"Is there something wrong with Michelle?" I asked, following her into her bedroom.

"Don't know yet. Go back to bed and don't wake Roy Boy."

Mom bent down and whispered something to Paw. He grumbled and rolled back over in bed, telling Mom to be careful.

I walked lightly back to my cot and prayed for Michelle. "God, please make her okay."

When the sun rose, Mom was still gone. Mrs. Derryhill had taken over her place in the kitchen. Mom had spoiled everyone in the camp, so they came to depend on her to provide early morning oatmeal and coffee. She told me she did this because we were the ones blessed with a large fireplace for cooking, so we needed to share our blessings with others.

Timmy rubbed his eyes and laid his head on the kitchen table while his mother prepared the food.

"Mrs. Derryhill, how did you know we needed help?" I asked.

"Your Paw came by my cabin in the wee hours of the morning and asked me to stay with you kids and get breakfast started. He wanted to be with your mom in case she needed help."

"That's nice."

"Just about ready," Mrs. Derryhill said as she slowly stirred the contents of the iron pot. "It'll thicken as it sits and cools."

The front door opened. Paw stood and looked a little uncomfortable about entering the kitchen area. I'll have to admit, it was an unsettled feeling to have Mrs. Derryhill in Mom's kitchen, wearing Mom's apron. I ran to where he stood and hugged him.

"Mornin', Dad."

"How's she doing?" Mrs. Derryhill asked, rapping the wooden spoon on the side of the pot to knock off a clump of oatmeal.

Paw removed his cap. "'Spose she's okay. Vinca's fixed some of her herbal concoctions, and she's resting."

"Vinca's quite knowledgeable about that herbal stuff, isn't she?" Mrs. Derryhill removed Mom's apron and hung it on the back of a chair.

"Yep. She likes her herbs and knows everything about 'em."

"Get yourselves something to eat, and I'll be on my way. Will you kids clean up when everyone's been served?"

No one said anything.

"Kids?" Paw asked.

"Sure Mrs. Derryhill. We'll clean it all up," Roy Boy answered.

When has Roy Boy ever helped with that before? I bet he'll leave it all for me to do.

"Real kind of you to help out this way, Diane. We appreciate it," Paw said.

"My pleasure. Just let me know if there's anything else

I can do." She wiped-down the small, wooden kitchen counter.

I didn't know your name was Diane. How about staying and washing the dishes, Diane?

"Hurry up, Timmy. We need to clean up so we can play," I ordered.

Timmy scraped the last of his oatmeal and placed the bowl and spoon in the sink. *Thanks a lot, Timmy. Feel free to clean your bowl.*

I heard the familiar knock at the front door— three short raps, followed by two more raps— meaning Mr. Chris had arrived to get his coffee. He didn't stick around to talk these days. I missed that. He left without even speaking to me. *What was going on with him?* By the end of the day, I would have my answer.

CHAPTER TEN

Mr. Chris' long arms remained crossed over his chest throughout dinner. His eyes lost the sparkle they once had and were now sunken and sullen. I felt sorry for him.

"Mr. Chris?" I said.

"Yeah, Effie?"

"Are you okay?"

"Yeah, Effie. I'll be okay. Nothing that a little vacation won't cure," he said.

"I thought this was vacation?"

He smiled. "You'll understand when you're older."

"I'll be eight soon. Will that be old enough to understand?"

He chuckled and rubbed my head. For a brief moment, the old Mr. Chris was back, and I liked it.

"I hate to see you so sad," I said.

"I'm not sad when I'm talking to you," he said, smiling. "You're the bright spot in this whole ordeal."

I didn't understand what an ordeal was, but I knew he just complimented me. "I'm glad I'm a bright spot in this ordeal, Mr. Chris. You can talk to me all you want if it makes you happy."

"You're funny, Effie. I'll miss seeing you around."

"Oh, Mom said we'll be at Marrying Tree for a while, so you don't have to worry about missing me any. That's what I've named this place . . . Marrying Tree. I'd best get ready for devotion time. I don't wanna be late."

Mr. Chris remained silent and didn't answer me back when I bid him farewell and gave him a quick hug. My face flushed, but he paid me no attention as I departed his presence.

I made sure I wasn't late for devotions that evening and actually arrived fifteen minutes early. Paw noticed and congratulated me for taking his admonishment seriously. My pride was overpowered by concern for Mr. Chris. He seemed distant, and no matter how much I smiled at him through Paw's lesson about Noah and the ark, the most I got in return was a cool nod, acknowledging my friendly gestures toward him.

That evening, after devotions, Roy Boy and I didn't feel like sleeping, so we headed up to Mr. Bantom's cabin where the grown-ups had their nightly meeting. We'd done this many times before and thought it was funny to see how differently they behaved when the kids weren't around. We were amused at their animation and to see that Mr. Derryhill could actually be funny. How strange to see him joke around so! He was stodgy and stoic during the day. I always thought Timmy was a chip off his father's block, but I could now tell he took after his mother and her persnickety ways.

When we arrived at the cabin, we assumed our usual spot under the open side window. We heard no talking for a minute until Mr. Chris spoke up.

"I don't know what else to say. I'm sick of this place, and I'm leaving."

I heard someone stomp their foot down hard on the floor.

"You cain't leave! End of discussion!" Paw shouted back. "We all swore to remain here until danger passed back home. You'll stay just like the rest of us."

"There isn't any danger, and you know it!" What I heard Mr. Chris say after this violated Paw's rule about no cussing. I was surprised to hear the anger in his tenor voice. They went at it back and forth until Mr. Bantom broke in. I took my hands off my ears and was glad the yelling stopped.

"You both need to simmer down and be reasonable for a moment. You're getting' the ladies upset. Now Chris —", Bantom said, pointing his thick finger at the young man, "You knew we'd be up here for a while, and you had a chance to stay in Burnt Willow. Right? Roy's tellin' the truth about people lookin' for us."

"I told you what I heard on the radio. People back home are getting worried and starting to hoard gasoline and weapons. The government's makin' all kinds of threats, tellin' people not to do it because it'll cause a shortage. Things are getting' rough," Paw said.

"I don't believe it," Mr. Chris grumbled.

Mr. Bantom took a deep breath and continued, "By now, there must be a posse out trying to figure out what happened to all of us. We can't take any chances having someone blab our whereabouts to the town folk."

"You won't have to worry about me talking to anyone about this rat hole," Chris said. "I'm sick of living here and want to go back. I'll take my chances about the so-called government intrusion in my life. I'm starting to think it was all a bunch of—"

Bantom interrupted. "Watch your language, Chris. We've heard enough tonight already. We get the picture."

"You can't leave. That's all there is to say about it. You made a commitment, Chris," Paw said.

Mr. Chris rose to his feet. "You all enjoy the rest of your meeting. I'm going to bed," he said as he turned and left the cabin.

I yanked Roy Boy's shirt and pulled him low to the ground so Mr. Chris wouldn't see us hiding. After the sound of his footsteps disappeared, we both slowly rose to the level of the window and peered over the sill. Paw nodded at Mr. Bantom. I saw Mr. Bantom stand and grab his shotgun as he walked out. I gasped.

"Shhhh! Be quiet, Effie!" Roy Boy whispered.

My only thoughts were about Mr. Chris' safety. I quietly walked to where I could see the front of Mr. Chris' cabin. Mr. Bantom sat on the ground outside, holding his shotgun. As far as I know, he remained there the rest of the evening, long after Roy Boy and I returned home to go to sleep.

• ● •

Beginning at dawn the next day, Mom kept vigil at Mike and Michelle's cabin and only left Michelle's side to take care of us. I helped Mom by bringing her the herbs she requested from home. I had become her "nursing assistant", as she called me, since I now was very well-versed on the properties of everything in her herbal arsenal.

"Keep drinking this," Mom said to Michelle. "You're probably gonna get tired of raspberry leaf tea, but it's good for pregnant women."

Michelle obediently sipped.

"Go tell the others that the cramping has stopped, and she's doing much better," Mom said to me. I ran and spread the word. Paw seemed happy when he heard my report about Michelle. That surprised me since he didn't want the baby in our camp.

"Your Mom is 'bout as close to having a doctor as we could ask for around here."

"Guess all that herb stuff works, huh, Paw?" Roy Boy said as he tied a string to his homemade kite.

"We're blessed to have someone who can take care of us like that," he answered. "Now go out and throw the garbage on the compost pile. I'm gonna go squirrel huntin'."

While Roy Boy finished his chores, I trailed along with Paw as far as Mr. Bantom's cabin.

"Do you have to shoot those poor little squirrels? They're so fluffy and cute."

"Now you go along and play if your work is done. No girls allowed on the huntin' trip. Bantom!" Paw called through the open cabin door. "You ready?"

I heard Mr. Bantom's voice but couldn't tell what he was saying. Apparently, Paw understood.

"How did that happen!" Paw shouted back. "You were there all night watchin'. Did ya fall asleep on the job?" Until last night, I'd never heard Paw raise his voice before in anger. Now he was doing it again.

"We'd better go see if we can find 'im." Paw stormed off the porch, nearly knocking me over. "Get otta the way, Lulu."

"What're you going to do, Paw?" I ran alongside him as he stomped toward Mr. Chris' cabin.

"Squirrel huntin'. I already told you that, Lulu. Now scram!" I wanted to enter Mr. Chris' cabin with Paw and Mr. Bantom, but Paw's command frightened me. "I said, scram, Lulu!"

"Please, God, keep Mr. Chris safe. Please God, keep him safe. Please God, keep him safe," I repeated all the way back home. Never before had I been so frightened.

Later in the afternoon, I heard one shot ring out. I stared at the edge of the woods hoping to see Paw carrying a dead squirrel. But his hands were empty when he appeared.

Paw entered the cabin, walking right past me without even saying a word. With a loud "plop" he fell on his bottom into a wooden dining room chair, where he sat for several minutes quietly, his steely eyes fixed straight ahead.

Mom took the teaball out of a steaming mug and carried the hot brew to Paw, who didn't look up at her. He took out his pocketknife and began scraping underneath his filthy fingernails.

"Sip on this. It'll calm you down. Chamomile."

"I hate the taste of all that stuff," he grumbled.

Mom sat across from him, opened her mouth to speak, but remained silent as she watched him continue digging with his pocketknife.

"Got any poison, Vinca?"

Mom started to rise from her seat, but Paw looked at her sternly.

"Stay right here a moment. I'm serious. Got any poison in all that stuff of yours?"

"What for?" Mom said. I could tell she was trying to stay calm, not to further rile him.

"For no good traitors," Paw said.

"Chris?" Mom asked.

Roy said nothing and stood as Mom's gaze followed him to the water barrel. Paw swished his hands in the sudsy water and wiped them on his pants.

"Come to your senses, Roy. You can't do something like that to another human. You shouldn't even be thinking of it. You're a Christian man."

"I'm afraid that protecting my family's my main concern right now." Paw walked back over to where Mom sat.

"He hasn't done anything to you."

"Not yet. But he will unless I stop him. Mix me up some of that skull stuff into some of that chamomile you're always pushing on me. Now do it! Leave it on the table tonight and I'll get it in the morning. I'm going to bed now."

Mom sat with her mouth open as if gasping for a breath. I looked at her, ready to scream at her if she dared mix up a poison concoction for my Mr. Chris. She mumbled so low I could barely hear her words, but I did catch the words, "Over my dead body."

No one heard or saw Mr. Chris again. Paw told us he must've taken off through the woods when Mr. Bantom went to the outhouse during the night. They searched most of the day of Mr. Chris' departure and half of the next before telling us it was a lost cause. I hoped Paw was speaking the truth about Mr. Chris' escape, but I just couldn't shake the memory of the shot I heard fired.

CHAPTER ELEVEN

After lunchtime, I made myself an extra sandwich out of Mom's wildberry jelly. I tucked Bear-Bear snuggly into the waistband of my shorts, along with my flashlight, and headed down the path toward the marrying tree. No one saw me leave, nor would anyone suspect anything if they were to run into me. I always played during this hour, so I figured I had plenty of time to find Mr. Chris. I'd taken many trips down the path as far as the marrying tree, sneaking further whenever no one else was with me. I felt confident I could guide him back to the camp if he'd gotten lost trying to find his way to where the cars had been left. The surrounding trees and brush had become familiar to me. Mom now allowed me to forage with Roy Boy, as long as we stayed on the path and didn't go past the marrying tree. Actually, I foraged and assigned his job to keep spiders and snakes away from me. We never had run into a snake on the path, but spiders flourished, unfortunately. This time, I was on my own. I felt my bravery slip away and become replaced with an uneasy feeling —a feeling that I was vulnerable to harm. The large web was strung from the branches of a small wild cherry tree to an elderberry bush and was within an arm's length from my face. I moved back very slowly and kept my eyes on the web until I was a safe distance away. *Guess I won't be picking any of those berries anytime soon.*

I felt my waistband to make sure Bear Bear was secure, before heading further down the path. If Mr. Chris had come this way, he would've gotten to the wide creek, and possibly crossed it by now.

The marrying tree stood tall and comforting about twenty steps ahead of me. As I approached its welcoming presence, my mind turned to Knock. The last time I saw him was here at the tree. He lived nearby. He said he did. I studied the area carefully, looking for any sign of a house.

"Maybe he's one of those elves who live in a tree," I said to myself, chuckling at the thought. My eyes wandered to each large tree, just in case. No doors on the trunks.

I pulled Bear Bear out of my waistband and held him tightly.

"We've got to find Mr. Chris. He can't make it alone in the woods. He doesn't know how to forage like we do. I bet he can't even cook."

My steps were slow and tentative as I continued down the hill. I'd only been this far with Mom twice since we'd moved to the camp, as she'd only taken me to the point where we could hear the creek rushing in the distance. I remembered her words of caution, "Don't go one step further than here. There might be someone fishing in the creek."

I didn't understand why that was a problem, but after

listening in on the adult meetings, I realized we were hiding out at Camp Marrying Tree.

"Marrying Tree," I said, rubbing its rough bark, "I've told you some secrets and you're supposed to make them come true. Right? Mr. Chris has to be okay because you promised he'd be my true love, right?" The tree's leaves gently rustled in the early autumn breeze. Its limbs were intertwined with another oak, forming a cool canopy overhead. I was glad I'd worn a long-sleeved shirt and corduroy jacket. Within the next month or so, the marrying tree's leaves would turn and fall to the ground. *I wonder what color the tree will be?* I hoped for orange. My second favorite color after purple. I smiled at the thought of a purple tree against a yummy orange sky.

I looked between the trees as far as I could see. As the limbs swayed, they cast bouncing shadows on the ground. Squirrels scurried, chasing each other around the trunk of a massive tree, chattering as they whirled in and out of my sight.

"Mr. Chris!" I called out, not using my loudest voice for fear of being heard at the camp. "Where are you?" I paused and listened for a response only to be met with the crackling sound of bark falling from a tree the squirrels played on.

I took ten steps down the hill, stopped and studied the perimeter again. Still no sign of Mr. Chris. I repeated this action five more times until I found myself at the broad creek, the one we crossed on our way to the camp four months ago. The water now rushed more briskly than I remembered the first morning I saw it. The recent rains caused the creek to be higher and fewer rocks poked through the surface. Mr. Chris would've had a difficult time getting across by himself, so I wondered if he wandered down the creek looking for a better place to cross. I pushed back some of the brambles and cautiously stepped around the branches in my way. As I leaned to avoid becoming entangled in a woody vine, Bear Bear toppled from my pocket and landed directly in the rushing stream of water in front of me.

I'm sure I must've screamed but wasn't aware because my mind was intent on saving my beloved Bear Bear from certain catastrophe. Not thinking clearly, I jumped into the dashing water and fell to my knees onto a jagged rock. I pulled myself to my feet and sloshed through the water as quickly as I could to catch Bear Bear. I finally spotted him caught in low-hanging brush along the shore of the creek ahead of me, so I held onto limbs and eased my way to where he bobbed up and down in the water. His small bandana was caught on some briars and prevented him from sailing down-creek.

I yanked hard and my little Bear Bear finally pulled loose from the prickly branch, leaving behind a tuft of his amber fur. I hugged him close to me and kissed his drenched head.

"I've got you, Bear Bear. Mommy will take care of you and not let anything bad happen to you." I kissed his head again and slipped him back into the waistband of my pants.

My shoes were heavy with water as I raised my feet out of the creek. I flopped onto the first clear spot I came to along the shore and took my shoes off. Small rocks and grit lay in the bottom of them. I scooted to the creek's edge and rinsed the offending pebbles out before squeezing my feet back into the snug sneakers. I shook as the air passed over my soaked body and wrapped my arms around my shoulders. How I wished I had dry clothes to wear!

I wasn't sure how far I'd traveled downstream, but knew I was far from anything familiar. Fear replaced the need to find Mr. Chris. I soon realized I was alone in the woods and didn't know how to get back to Camp Marrying Tree. I rose and looked at my immediate surroundings. Nettles and some unrecognizable brush to my left; laurel and oaks to my right. *Is that a fishing spider on the ground next to me?!* I screamed at the sight of the huge arachnid and moved slowly away from its brown, furry body. It ran underneath a leaf on the ground. I reached up under my wet sleeve, scratched my arm and sobbed. I was comforted to feel Bear Bear, cold and wet, tucked close to me.

I found a sunny spot next to the creek and basked in the tiny amount of warmth radiating off the earth beneath me. The bottom half of my pants and sleeves were wet and clung to my chilled skin. My body trembled as a breeze blew over. I wrapped my arms tightly around my legs, pulling them close to my chest.

"Paw! Mom!" I yelled at the top of my lungs. The sound of my own frightened voice calling out was eerie to me. No one answered back. Only the chattering of squirrels and the sound of the rushing creek broke the silence. *Surely Mom and Paw will find me soon.*

My growling stomach, as well as the disappearing sun, told me it was dinner time back at camp. Mom was making a new soup recipe tonight. "Fall Harvest Porridge" she named it. I was looking forward to tasting it even though I had no idea what ingredients she was using. *Onions?*

Maybe. Yes, there were some left. I saw them in the pantry. Carrots? Possibly. Kale? Yuk. I hope not. I remembered the large amount of potatoes we dug just the other day. Certainly there would be potatoes in the Fall Harvest Porridge. *What meat will she put in it?* I wondered if one of the chickens would be killed for the soup. Those were used very sparingly.

My mind drifted back to the time a few days ago when Paw killed a chicken. I was out playing by the creek with Roy Boy. I think he purposely waited until we were gone before doing the deed.

"I can't stand to see a girl cry," I'd heard Paw say on a couple occasions.

Yes, I would've cried. When Roy Boy and I returned to the cabin, there it was, plopped on the kitchen counter — a dead chicken. Half-plucked, it was difficult to tell who it was. *Clucky? Could be. Maybe Chicken Little?* That one chased me around the pen every time I took feed to them.

"Do you want to help me pluck the chicken?" I remembered Mom asking me that day. *Is she crazy?*

I stood horrified as Mom pulled the feathers out of the poor chicken. That night, Tippy got my portion of chicken, on the sly, of course. There was no way I was going to swallow one bite of whoever-it-was.

I took inventory the next morning. *Definitely Chicken Little.* I think he was missing because all of the remaining chickens were well-behaved. Or maybe they knew their turn could be next and were just laying low. I walked behind the outhouse and cried about Chicken Little. He couldn't help it if he was mean; that's the way God created him. I still didn't want him to die. I said a prayer and sang a hymn softly, just like everyone did at my grandfather's funeral a few years earlier. Even though I was quite young when he passed away, I remembered it.

Paw never learned how upset I was over the chicken. I kept a brave face whenever I was around him. However, my stomach did a flip each time he approached the chicken pen.

I shook off the thought of that day, and suddenly didn't feel so strong. The creek rushed past me, making me feel even colder as it gurgled around the rocks.

"Paw!" I yelled again. I paused and waited to see if there was a response but heard none.

Which direction did I come from?

Without hesitation, I stood and climbed the creek bank and surveyed my surroundings. Only the very tops of the trees now captured the sun's deep gold rays. Very soon, it would be completely dark.

With a large stick in hand, I cut through the brush, and headed back toward where I thought camp must be located. Panic gripped me. I recognized nothing. I pushed myself to run faster and faster in the direction of the sunset.

The sound of a gunshot in the distance frightened me. I ran further into the woods, hacking at the brush and spider webs with my stick. No stranger was going to nab me. Paw's words about people coming after us flashed through my mind. *Was this Martial Law looking for me? Paw said Martial Law didn't want any of us out after dark and would take our rations away.*

As my eyes adjusted to the darkened surroundings, I saw a large oak ahead with very little brush around it. I stumbled my way toward it, as it looked like a safe place to rest and collect my thoughts. I swiped my stick completely around the perimeter before settling down to sit on a large exposed root. There was no use continuing to look for camp. Despite my best effort to find it, I resolved that I was hopelessly lost. The woods would have to be my home tonight.

I sat as closely as I could to the massive trunk of the tree and pretended it was Paw. Salty tears ran down my face. My tongue captured them as they spilled across my lips. I reached for Bear Bear, but my waistband was empty. I'd dropped him somewhere along the way and panicked.

"Bear Bear . . ." I was horrified at the thought of my little Bear Bear alone in the woods without me. Now I was truly alone. I pushed my sleeves up and scratched my arms raw.

"Paw?" I said weakly. Was there any use in calling out his name again, I wondered?

What if some mountain man finds me and takes me to his cabin and locks me in a cage? I scratched my arms. *I'll be very quiet and won't take any chances. I won't yell, and I won't try to find camp tonight. First thing in the morning, I'll start looking again.*

I wanted to scream so loudly at every rustle I heard. *Was that an owl? Or maybe a coyote?* Something made a screeching noise, and I didn't like it one bit.

Clouds passed quietly across the rising moon. The higher the moon got, the brighter it shone, until the woods appeared to have a light dusting of snow on every exposed surface. The moon caused me to feel as if I were being looked after by the radiant face of God, Himself. In that, I found some comfort. I wondered if Mom was sad and crying. Paw, I figured was either very frightened or angrier than ever at me. If it was the latter, there'd be a whipping, for sure. *Maybe they'll be so happy to see me they won't punish me.*

Another rustling through the leaves moved closer. I took my jacket and pulled it completely over my head, keeping my arms in the sleeves, remaining as still as a dead man. With my coat covering my eyes, I could pretend to be anywhere. I told myself I was safely tucked under the blanket on my bed. Or maybe I was camping in the woods with Paw and Roy Boy. *That's why there's a cool breeze blowing over me. The campfire has gone out and someone forgot to zip the tent closed.*

I rested my arms on the tree's trunk and leaned my head against it, still covered.

"Paw, I'm sure glad you're here with me," I whispered. "You'll keep me safe."

My eyes grew tired, but I fought back sleep. *What if no one ever finds me? I may never see Mom or Paw again.* It even made me sad to think of not growing up with Roy Boy. *And Tippy. Tippy would wonder where I was.* My sleepy brain conjured up thoughts of our family reunions back in Burnt Willow. Uncle Rick, my favorite uncle, would certainly grieve the loss of his "favorite niece", as he called me. Of course, I always reminded him that I was his only niece. But it still made me feel good to be called anyone's favorite.

I would hide behind Mom when he came to the door of our house.

"Where's Davis?" he'd ask first thing.

I'd leap out from behind Mom. He pretended to be surprised.

"That can't be Davis! Davis is a tiny little thing with dirt on her clothes and a pacifier in her mouth. What I see is a beautiful young lady!"

I'd run up to him and hug him tightly. "You know my name isn't Davis!" He expected me to repeat this line every time we met.

"Your name's Effie D. So I thought the 'D' stood for Davis." He'd laugh and wait for my next line.

"Dee IS my middle name! You know that. It ain't Davis!"

How I loved Uncle Rick. I couldn't bear the thought of not seeing him again, and I was sure he would feel the same. I was his favorite niece, after all.

I sobbed until sleep overtook me.

CHAPTER TWELVE

When I awoke, I took a chance and pulled the jacket down from my eyes only to see that the faintest bit of light had turned the black canopy into a deep royal blue. Only one or two of the very brightest stars still appeared in the sky between the black branches above. The rest had miraculously faded into wherever they hid during the day. *Where do all the stars go when the sun rises?*

Although nervous, my stomach still told me to feed it. My eyes adjusted to my shadowy surroundings, so I could now make out the shape of various plants in my vicinity. Spider webs still clung to most of the plants I touched. I recoiled and shook my hands trying to get the clinging strands off, only succeeding by rubbing my fingers along the rough bark of a nearby tree. *Where's my Bear Bear? I have to find him.*

I sat still so I wouldn't end up getting caught in a spider's web, having it completely suck the juices out of me.

Mom must be fixing breakfast back at the camp. I

could see her standing at the fire, slowly stirring the cast iron pot of oatmeal. My stomach growled as I remembered the smell of the freshly-baked bread which was always sitting on the table waiting to be slathered with butter.

"Ef," she'd say as I sat on a stool in front of the hearth. "Stand here and stir this for me so it won't stick to the bottom. I felt so grown up and hoped someone would come through the door seeing me cook.

Boy, I could go for some of that oatmeal right now. My stomach's growling grew louder. The leaves on a low-growing plant a few feet away looked tempting. I remembered Mom tossing some like this in the salads she'd fix for dinner. I moved in closely and surveyed the area. Seemed to be spider free, so I tentatively reached my hand down and pulled a clump of leaves off the spindly plant. I wiped them on my jacket and put one in my mouth. Tangy and very bitter. I salivated and wished for a drink of cool water, but the river was way back through the trees and I'm not even sure I could find it again if I tried. Some berries clung to the branches of a tall bush. I wasn't quite sure what they were, but I determined that God must've created them for someone to enjoy. I pulled one off the bush and popped it into my mouth. Maybe pokeberries? Mom had harvested leaves from poke in the past and used them. The berries practically fell from the branch as I pulled it toward me. *I'll save the rest for lunch,* I decided, shoving them into my jacket pocket.

Even though I was terribly hungry, my main concern was Bear Bear. He was missing and I needed his presence desperately. A month prior, Paw taught me to track animals by looking for brush that had been mashed down. I figured maybe I could retrace my steps using this method, so I turned to my right and followed a narrow path where I spied some broken twigs on the ground. Yes. This area looked familiar to me. I had, indeed, passed the dead tree with the large bulge halfway down its trunk. And there was the hole my foot slipped into yesterday evening. I don't know what made me look but sitting against the bottom of a nearby hickory was my little Bear Bear. He looked as if he had been carefully placed there. His tawny fur blended in with the base of the tree. Large roots cradled him on either side. I squatted down to where he sat, looked for spiders and snatched him up into my arms.

"I didn't mean to leave you behind my baby Bear Bear. I hope you weren't scared." I held the small doll close and continued to retrace my steps through the woods. I thought.

As the afternoon gained warmth, the clouds quickly formed and darkened. Distant rumbles of thunder grew in intensity until one huge clap sent me seeking the shelter of a boulder I viewed about 20 feet downhill of where I stood. I held Bear Bear tightly to my chest. He felt slightly damp and smelled of wet dog. Just as I always suspected, Tippy had played with him when I wasn't around. I wondered how many times I'd unfairly accused Roy Boy of hiding him from me when it had actually been the dog.

With my nose burrowed into Bear Bear's moist fur, I drew in a long breath and savored the familiar aroma of Tippy. I was momentarily transported to last summer. Me, playing in the back yard with the green garden hose as Tippy nipped at the arched stream of cool water. Tippy's fur would be hot and steamy as he ran around the yard, chasing the water. I'd squirt him, then he'd tackle me, sending me to the grassy ground as he dashed around and around before shaking the water off his fur.

"Ew! Get away from me, Tippy!" I'd yell. "You stink to high heavens!"

What I'd give to have him near me now. I'd take a thousand times a smelly Tippy over the loneliness of being lost in the woods.

The wind picked up and felt refreshing on my face. I lapped at the chilly stream of air, pretending it to be cascading water from the hose. I could almost smell the sweet fragrance of moist earth. I closed my eyes and filled my lungs one, two, three times, in and out. As if my thoughts were coming to life, I heard pattering noises all around as rain began to fall through the thick canopy of tree branches above me. A brilliant flash crossed the smoky sky, followed by a sound like bowling pins being struck by a zipping ball, crashing to the hard ground. This was serious rain. Not a quick shower that satisfies after a hot afternoon. I peeked out from under the boulder's overhang and noticed there was no blue sky to be seen.

I was tired, scared, and hungry. I'd been holding in the tears all morning, but couldn't anymore, so I let them flow until my sobs turned to anguished heaves. *Will I ever see Paw or Mom again? Why haven't they come after me?* I had never felt so helpless before in my life, which in itself was a marvel. Mom had always said I was a bit of a loner and that my imagination was my best friend. But that was no reason to leave your child alone in the woods.

I wept because I missed my parents. I wept because I wanted to be protected. I wept because I wanted dry clothes. I wept because I wanted food for my hollow stomach. And, yes, I even wept because I wanted to see Roy Boy.

A large branch cracked off a tree and hung in the limbs of another, rocking back and forth in the wind. The rain grew harder and harder, pelting the treetops. I never realized how loud rain could be. The rock offered some protection when the wind blew from behind, but very little otherwise. Streams of water ran down my scalp and mixed with the salty tears on my face. I stuck my tongue out and licked at the saltiness, which tasted good — the first salt I'd tasted in a while. Another stream trickled from the behind my ear, ran down my neck and soaked the back of my shirt. I pulled my clothes closer around me, then brushed my wet, matted hair out of my face.

I twisted the bottom of my rain-soaked shirt and sucked the water out of the fabric. The water was sweet and delicious to my thirsty mouth. As the rain poured, I cupped my hands and caught as much as I could, sipping eagerly from my grimy palms. The water offered little relief to my grumbling stomach, which had not had a meal in a little over a day. I remembered the berries I'd collected earlier, so my fingers eagerly scrambled around in my pocket to find them. To my surprise, I located three shriveled blackberries, and a few of what I believed to be pokeberries, in my other coat pocket so I popped those into my mouth and chewed them up. I nearly forgot to pray for my meal.

"Thank You, God, for this food. And God, please make it quit raining and help me to find my Paw. I'm scared, God. Amen."

I held the suspected pokeberries out in the rain to rinse them and bit down on them hard. My teeth pierced the rubbery skins, sending the sweet-tangy juice throughout my mouth. The taste turned foul as I swirled it around my tongue. Hard, woody seeds were impenetrable to my bite, so I spit them out one by one. I shivered a little as I chewed up the skins and swallowed. Some pulp remained in my mouth, so I spit it out into a passing stream of water. I lifted my face to the falling rain and marveled at how wonderful it tasted on my sour tongue. I rinsed the bad aftertaste out of my mouth and allowed my red saliva to spill to the ground. I watched as the flowing rainwater carried my red spittle with it, diluting it as it traveled along. I kept spitting, thinking it was neat to watch. My mind filled with memories of the old movie about Moses when the water in Pharaoh's palace mixed with blood, turning all of the water bright red. That scene gave me nightmares for weeks when I was five.

Where's my Paw? I want Paw and Mom.

"God? I know you hear me anytime I talk to You. Please help. I wanna be out of these woods. It scares me. I ain't never been so scared in all my life. And I'm hungry. And my tummy's hurting so bad. Amen."

I cried and doubled over in pain, sobbing as I began heaving. I barely got my pants pulled down over my knees before the diarrhea started. Squatting over a mud puddle, I thought I was going to die right there, and no one would ever know what happened to me. My body would be consumed by the wild animals of the forest. I sobbed, threw up and passed watery stools over the next hour until my body was drained of everything it held. My strength was spent. I struggled to pull up my drenched pants, budging them only a little.

All I could think of was sleeping. I waddled back to the

rocky overhang, my twisted pants cut into my chapped, icy thighs. I made one more attempt at pulling my pants up, moving them enough to barely cover my bottom, then removed my soaked jacket. The jacket made a poor pillow under my head, but I was so tired that I didn't care if it was lumpy and wet. I laid my limp body down on the cold, muddy ground and curled into a tight ball. My rain-soaked clothing offered me no warmth against the hard, pelting shower.

As I lay still, half asleep, I sensed a presence and heard footsteps crunching in the rocky sludge nearby. At this point, I welcomed the thought of a bear finishing me off, ending my misery. The fact was, I hadn't the energy to run or fight. I peeked through leaden eyelids and saw the shape of a person standing in front of me. *Am I dreaming?*

"Paw?" I squeaked. If the person answered, I couldn't hear it through the sound of the rain. I felt a hand brushing my hair softly.

"Paw? Is that you? Take me home, Paw."

The figure of a man bent down closer, and the strangest thing happened. Although the rain was deafening now, I clearly heard the words, "Don't fear. Your Paw will find you shortly." With those words, I felt my body relax and realized I was looking into Knock's gentle, blue eyes, consoling at me with the kindest look anyone ever gave me. My Knock, the one who would always take care of me when I was in trouble.

He wrapped me in a blanket and tucked Bear Bear next to my face. Nothing had ever felt so warm. I don't know how that blanket stayed dry, nor Bear Bear for that matter. All I cared about was the knowledge that Paw was on his way to get me. And that I was very, very tired and wanted to sleep.

When I awoke, I was inside my cabin at Camp Marrying Tree. Mom, Paw, and Roy Boy surrounded me. Mom sat in her chair reading a book. Paw reached over and nudged her on the shoulder, nodding in my direction. Mom let out a gasp and squeezed me so hard I thought I would break in two, but I didn't care. Her arms were the most wonderful things I'd ever felt!

"Welcome home, Lulu," Paw said, sitting down on the edge of my cot. "My little Lulu."

I know I saw tears well up in his eyes. He turned his head away from me for a moment and wiped his eyes with his sleeve. When he looked at me again, he let out a loud "whoop!"

Roy Boy's lip was quivering. I saw his I'm-not-going-to-cry look. I'd seen it many times before. He remained silent with his eyes fixed on mine. I was touched that he seemed so relieved to see me.

"We thought you were gone forever," Paw said, before completely breaking down, sobbing. He held his head in his hand while Mom stroked his back lovingly.

"Praise God," Mom whispered, grabbing Paw's hand tightly. "We've got our baby back."

I must've fallen back to sleep because the next thing I remember was lying on the cot with a horribly foggy head.

Paw was no longer sitting by my bedside but stood by the fireplace watching me intently. Mom explained how I'd been found in the woods the previous day, which confused me tremendously before realizing I'd slept through one whole night and part of the current day. *Hadn't I just seen Knock?* That was the last thing I remembered from the woods.

"You were right at the edge of the camp, out cold," Paw told me. "Don't know how we missed findin' you. We looked and looked all over the place. Everyone in the camp did."

"I was in the woods," I whispered back, licking my parched lips.

"You were in the woods all that time?" Mom asked. "With nothing to eat?"

I nodded.

"But you had to see the camp because you were right there within sight when we found you."

"I never saw the camp."

"You mean you was right there and didn't see the cabin? That don't make any sense. I could've thrown a rock and hit you, you was so close. You must've crawled your way there," Paw said.

"I ain't fibbing. Really, Paw. I was in the woods all that time."

"Now, Paw, don't quiz her like that. You're going to upset her. She's telling the truth if she says she didn't see us. It's not like her to make up things."

Paw gave Mom "the look".

"If you're thinking about her make-believe friends, that doesn't count," Mom said to him. "That's different than being a liar. Effie doesn't lie."

"I wasn't accusing her of being a liar. It's just strange that she didn't see the camp. Lulu, I'm so glad you're home," he said, squeezing my arm.

"Your Paw and I were worried sick. He's not mad at you. He's just trying to understand what happened."

"I lost Bear Bear. I dropped him in the river and had to chase him," I told them.

"You mean you got lost chasing after a stupid stuffed animal?" Roy Boy said. "That's really dumb."

Mom shushed him and looked at me, a puzzled expression on her face.

"How did you get wrapped in that blanket? You couldn't have walked being wrapped so tightly."

"Knock did it, I think."

There was that look again between Paw and Mom.

"Knock told me you were on your way to get me. I'm sure he wrapped me."

"We'll have to thank him when we see him," Mom mumbled.

"Now where exactly is it he lives?" Paw asked. "In a cabin in the woods . . . or maybe a tree stump?"

Did I sense sarcasm in his voice? "He didn't tell me. But I don't think he lives in a tree. Paw, don't you believe me?"

"He believes you, baby," Mom said, tucking the blanket around my feet. "Now what can I get you to eat? Some soup?"

I nodded and sat up. Mom filled my favorite green bowl with the most marvelous sight I'd seen in days— steaming, cooked food! Paw remained propped against the wall next to the fireplace, tapping his finger against his chin like he always did when deep in thought.

"Careful, Effie. I just cooked it and it's still very hot."

I didn't care if I burned my mouth. That soup couldn't get into my stomach quickly enough to suit me. I felt the heat travel down my esophagus and coat the inside of my belly, sending a wave of warmth over my entire body. How wonderful it felt to be warm and dry! My spoon eagerly scraped at the bottom of the bowl. I placed the bowl against my lips and tipped it, sipping the last of the broth.

"That's the best soup I've ever tasted! What kind is it?"

"Chicken. Just like I always make," Mom said. "You're just very hungry."

"What's wrong, Mom?" Mom had turned away from me and bent her head over. I think she didn't want me to see her cry.

"I can't stand the thought of my baby being in the woods lost and hungry. I was crazy frightened about you, Effie." Mom sat down next to my cot and draped her arms around my neck. She held me for a long time before I felt her weight slip away from me and saw her slowly collapse to the floor. Mom was sound asleep. Her breathing was soft and steady; her face looked serene. I wondered if she had slept at all since I disappeared.

CHAPTER THIRTEEN

—•●•—

I sat at the wooden table in the kitchen area, while Mom bent over scooping ash from the fireplace with the small wrought iron shovel.

"Chamomile, yum, spearmint, yum, sugar, no smell but yum, yum, licorice root, okay, sassafras, yum, boneface poison, yuck, . . ." I held the jar under my nose and drew in its woodsy aroma. "Too bad you're not good for me because you kind of smell good," I said, taking another look at the poison symbol, just to make sure. "Feverfew, burdock, lavender." I continued naming Mom's herbs and powders by sniffing them, then by sight if I was stumped. Her collection of herbs had grown in the last couple of months of foraging, so there were more things to quiz me on. Mom walked to the table and rearranged the thirty jars once more. I proceeded to repeat the process.

"What's this one used for?" I said, tapping the side of the jar.

Mom leaned in and sniffed. "I make a poultice out of that one. That's one you don't want to ingest. But if you get a boo-boo, it's a good one to have around. And the boneface poison is to kill off vermin." She continued to clean.

"What's a vermin?"

"Vermin is anything that gets into our garden or supplies and ruins them or eats them. Like rats and bugs mostly. Pests."

"What about when the rabbits were eating our vegetables in the garden? Were they vermin?" I asked.

"Yes. Before we got wise and built a fence around vegetables, they certainly were vermin," she answered.

"Did you give them boneface poison and make them die?"

"I started to, but then remembered they wouldn't be good for eatin' if I poisoned them."

Mom looked at my sad face, "Don't worry, honey. I haven't cooked one yet. But if they start burrowing under the fence, I can make no promises."

I didn't like the way she said "yet" and "no promises". There was no way I'd ever eat a rabbit or any other cute animal. I ate chickens, but they weren't particularly cute, however, I did still feel sorry for Chicken Little.

"Mom? Is Mr. Chris back yet?"

Mom was quiet for a moment before answering. "Honey, he won't be back."

She kept her head down and didn't look me in the eyes. Mom pushed her hair away from her face and walked to the pantry door, opened it and pulled out a bucket of wheat. She placed it on the floor next to the table and yanked hard on the lid. It didn't budge.

I ran to the bucket and helped her pull until the edges of the lid began to lift off.

"My, you're strong, aren't you?" Mom said, smiling.

I went back to my stool and stared at her as she scooped wheat berries into a large bowl. She glanced up briefly, long enough to see my eyes on her, then put her full attention on the grain mill which stayed clamped to the edge of the worktable. I was determined to know the truth about Mr. Chris and wasn't going to let her skirt the subject.

"Where'd he go?" I said, watching her expression carefully while I held back tears.

"Who?"

How could she forget who we were talking about so quickly?

"Mr. Chris. Mom, where'd he go to? Did he go back home?"

"I reckon that's just where he went, Honey. Now go play and let me grind the wheat in peace. Roy Boy was looking for you earlier, so why don't you go find him."

How strange. Mom always likes to have company when she makes bread.

I left and went outside to where Roy Boy and Timmy sat on the ground, digging out small trenches with a stick. Roy Boy "ka-powed!" loudly two times, and Timmy threw small pebbles at larger rocks which were embedded in the dirt.

"Go away. No girls allowed," Roy Boy growled at me. Timmy cowered a little, probably not wanting to get caught in the coming crossfire between me and Roy Boy. "We're playing war, so scam!"

Before I had a chance to clobber him, Timmy spoke up. "Let her stay! We need enemies to blow up."

Timmy was becoming quite the diplomat. I was

impressed at his newfound skills in brokering a deal to allow me to stay and join the game.

"Well, since you put it that way . . ."

We played in the dirt, only taking a break to eat a quick lunch before getting back to our game. As the sun became low in the sky, an ominous feeling came over me — a feeling that disturbed me and clung to me as my wet, cold clothes clung to my body while lost in the woods. My intuition was speaking and demanded my attention. Something was afoot. Something I didn't understand. Something I felt I needed to explore further.

* * *

After I was supposed to be tightly tucked in bed, I crept to the meeting tent where Paw and Mr. Bantom went over the day's activities, as was their custom. This was the same tent I sat in two hours earlier, listening to the nightly devotional about Moses and Nehemiah. Paw told us how he believed he had been appointed by God to lead us into safety. I'd never heard Paw speak so strongly about himself and so little about the Bible. Maybe I was mistaken, but I felt as if everyone else was as uncomfortable as I, while he rambled on about being obedient to our leader, and how by being obedient to him, we were doing God's will. I saw the looks on their faces and noticed how they fidgeted in their chairs. At one time during Paw's speech, Mrs. Derryhill whispered something to Timmy. The smile on his face quickly disappeared.

Now, Paw spoke with Mr. Bantom and, as much as I feared what I might hear, I couldn't leave the spot outside the open window. I watched Paw's shadow on the wall as he leaned toward Bantom, pointing a finger at his face.

"You'd better be in agreement that anyone leaving the camp for any reason at all will be chased down and dealt with. And know this Bantom, if you get a wild hair and decide to go into town without letting me know, like you did last week, I'll be coming after you with a shotgun in my hand."

"Calm yourself down, Roy. No one saw me. I wanted to see what was going on in the real world. And for your information, nothing was. Your prophecy of gloom and doom has been a lot of hot air, just like your threats. I swung by your garage that night and saw a light on inside."

"You shouldn't a gone by there. People are probably waiting to see if I come back."

"Have you gone back there, Roy?" Mr. Bantom asked sternly. "I think you're creeping back into town yourself Pomeroy. Maybe someone should watch you carefully and chase you down. What do you think?"

Paw was quiet, then snorted a little. "You don't know what you're talking about. I think we have a bigger threat closer than you know. That Knock Effie's always talking about. She didn't just get back to camp by herself that day. And how could she have wrapped herself up in a blanket like that? Weren't even my blanket! No, he ain't a figment of her imagination. There's really someone out there watching us. And as soon as martial law comes down on everyone, they'll be all over us like a swarm of bees. They were talking on the radio about it last night. It's getting' close."

"There ain't gonna be no martial law, Roy, and you know it. I believed you for a while, but now I know better. We're all free to leave, and nothing's gonna happen to us back home," Bantom said. "Let 'em go back, Roy. Let 'em go."

"Just let' em try, Bantom . . . just you try, yourself, and see what I do. End of discussion."

"You love these people. You wouldn't harm them if they wanted to go home. Some of 'em are your own blood. You can't hold everyone here forever. Don't make me tell Vinca about our agreement. Don't make me tell her that you're keeping her up here because you made a costly mistake."

"I certainly wouldn't want you to . . ." Paw's voice drifted off. I couldn't understand the next thing he said.

I wanted to throw up. My Paw, the one who loves me more than life itself, had changed. I didn't know the person inside that tent. I wanted my mother's arms around me so badly, but I couldn't tell her what I'd heard or where I'd been. Never.

Later that night, I saw Paw sneak off to his secret spot on the other side of camp, with the radio in his hands. He said the reception on his old transistor radio was better over there. I wondered if, on his nightly news program, they were saying scary things about people chasing after innocent families, like ours. Families who were just trying to stay safe and take care of each other. Families who, like Paw told us a million times, were just wanting the government to stay out of their business and live peacefully.

CHAPTER FOURTEEN

When the sun rose, I didn't want to get out of bed. I had not slept at all through the night and now the comfort of daylight made me feel more at ease and safe enough to close my eyes. My sleep, however, was short-lived. I heard Paw talking to Mom as they drank their morning cup of coffee.

Mom called me and Roy Boy to the table to eat breakfast. I sat down across from Paw, in my usual place, and began to eat my pancake. I studied Paw's face. My stare was caught by him, causing me to turn my eyes away quickly. I felt uncomfortable, afraid that my father could read my thoughts or sense the fear I was feeling. Fearing my father was something new to me. I hoped I was being too hard on him and had misunderstood what I heard him express in his conversation with Mr. Bantom the previous night. Surely Paw had our safety in mind and was just trying to scare Mr. Bantom.

Clearly, Paw had something on his mind. I could tell by his silence. He turned his sullen gaze toward Mom, watching her wipe down the griddle. He rubbed the stubble on his chin over and over, then sipped his coffee slowly. His spoon twirled nervously in his fingers, then he banged it down on the table. Normally, Paw would've teased me a couple of times or pulled my nose by now, but he hardly acknowledged my presence.

I watched Roy Boy as he poked a design in his pancake with the prongs of his fork. He held the plate up so Paw and I could admire his handiwork. Paw finally broke his silence.

"You gonna eat that or just play with it?"

Roy Boy looked at me. I shrugged.

"Food might get scarce. Then you're gonna wish you had that pancake to eat."

I waited for Mom to interject her usual, "Don't scare the kids", but she kept silent. Paw downed the last bit of his coffee, wiped his mouth, and threw his napkin down onto the table.

"Got a heap of work to get done before the weather turns colder. Got all your canning done, Vinca?"

"Pretty much," was her only reply. She sat at the table with us and pulled her apron off over her head.

"Looks like it might be a stormy day," she said. "You all had better make hay while the sun shines."

Paw cracked the first hint of a smile. "Ain't no sunshine out there. But I'd better go finish the caulkin' on Mike and Michelle's cabin."

Paw exited the cabin, letting the door slam behind him.

"Paw mad about something?" I asked Mom.

"He's been a little tense lately, for sure. Got a lot on his mind.

"Are we gonna starve, Mom?"

"Of course not! Have you seen all the jars of food in the closet and storage building? And you know the Bible tells us that God will take care of our needs better than He takes care of the needs of the birds and other creatures."

"Why did Paw say we were gonna want our pancakes this winter? Don't he believe God'll take care of us?"

"Well, when you're a father, you feel responsible for your family, and sometimes you might forget that everything isn't your responsibility," she explained.

"Oh. Like keeping us safe?"

Mom remained quiet but nodded slowly.

"Is Paw keeping us safe or is God keeping us safe?" I asked.

Mom paused for a moment before answering. "Good question, Effie," she said softly. Mom cleared away the breakfast dishes and continued talking, barely audible, as if she were speaking to herself. "I suppose Paw intends to keep us safe, but it's really God Who has the final word about it. If we're in God's hands, we're truly safe. No matter what happens."

I didn't completely understand Mom's response to me. She may have meant for her words to be comforting, but they didn't accomplish their purpose.

"Roy Boy, go see if you can help your Paw. And Effie, you can dry dishes and put them away."

I grabbed a dishcloth and stood ready while Mom filled the sink with sudsy water.

"By the way," I said, "I switched two of your dried herbs around. Can you guess which ones? Now it's my turn to test you!"

Mom turned off the water and left the dishes in the sink

to soak. She seemed concerned when she saw me lifting the lids to her herb canisters, one by one, my face must've betrayed my confusion.

"Mom, this don't smell like chamomile, and this one don't smell like spearmint, and this bonehead stuff don't smell like . . . "

"Leave all of that alone now. I don't want you touching these anymore."

I didn't understand why Mom messed up all the jars. Could've been a game she planned to play with me, but somehow it worried me to see her herbs all messed up. That wasn't like Mom at all.

"Do you want me to put everything back where they belong, Mom?"

"No. I just don't want you messing with the herbs anymore."

"I haven't been messing with them. Did Roy Boy do this?" I asked.

"No, Honey. I'm thinking about rearranging them in different canisters permanently, so they fit better."

I could tell something wasn't right with Mom. Her words weren't coming out of her mouth in a sincere way. She sounded like I do when I'm trying to pull a fast one over on her. And whenever she calls me "Honey", I know there's something on her mind.

"Now, see if you can tell what's in the canisters without the labels," Mom said. "I'll give you a hint." She opened the lids of two canisters and held them under My nose. "I switched your number one favorite and your number seven favorite."

"Let's see . . . you swapped spearmint and verbena!"

"Right! Good job! I'll test you again later on. It'll be a surprise."

"Let me mix some up and you can guess!" I eagerly said.

"I'd rather you not mix my herbs around, Honey, or you might end up making feverfew tea instead of Chamomile."

"Yuck! I wouldn't like that at all."

Mom motioned to me to come to her and start drying dishes. "Rinse your hands off first, Honey."

"Smelling that spearmint sure was making me thirsty!"

"Not yet. You have a job to do here, Mom replied. "Maybe you can have some number one favorite tea after you're finished."

Paw and Mr. Bantom managed to get our old transistor radio running again. It died right after Paw got his last news update. The radio was kept in a carefully guarded, secret location in camp. Paw told me he kept it hidden because he didn't want kids playing with it and running the batteries down. What Paw didn't know is that I found out where he kept the radio hidden and used it many times to listen to music when no one was around. I once saw him shove it back into an old satchel and place it in the small outbuilding with our gardening tools.

Paw sat at the picnic table fiddling with the radio to test it out. He stood and walked to the clearing in front of the cabin then turned his eyes skyward as he held the radio to his ear. I could not hear what was being said but Paw seemed to be giving the announcer his full attention, shaking his head at the news.

"Oh, boy," was all I heard him say as he turned off the radio.

Curiosity got the best of me, so I approached Paw, apprehensively, to see what the trouble was. "Martial law, Paw?"

"No, Lulu. Bad weather's headed this way."

"What kind of bad weather?" I asked.

"Fierce lightning, high winds, and maybe hail. It's blowing in over the mountains tonight and headin' straight our way."

Paw gathered together the men and got them started making repairs to cabin roofs. A couple of cabins still had partially tarped roofs, so he and Mike got busy shingling, which was a job they began earlier in the summer and never completed. He instructed Mom to have the women cover the chicken pens with tarps, staking them down to secure them to the ground. She and the other women carried pieces of equipment to the cabin porches in order to keep them somewhat dry. Barrels were uncovered to catch the precious rain, which served as a source of drinking water for the camp. Mom said she was excited about the storm coming and producing several inches of her "good water". This was the kind of water she prefered to wash our hair and clothing in, saying it made them softer. We had to settle for creek water during the dry spells.

Darkness fell over the camp, and because everyone was so exhausted, we skipped the usual evening devotion time and went straight to bed. It promised to be a bumpy night, so sleep might be short-lived. Paw reminded us that there would surely be some clean-up work in the morning after the storm, and if any trees fell, they would need to be cut up. Because we cooked most of our food over fires, we almost hoped for a few fallen trees – away from the cabins, of course. We used the generator as sparingly as possible and only for special things, as gasoline was a precious commodity; firewood was usually plentiful and sufficient for our current needs.

I kept my cover pulled over my face for most of the night. At some point, however, I relented to my tired body's cry for sleep. No longer did I let the constant flashes blasting through the cabin's window scare me. Strangely, the pelting cadence on the tin roof comforted me and drowned out some of the rumbles of thunder.

I don't know if it was late at night or very early in the morning – the darkness deceived me – when the household was awakened by a large blast, followed by pounding on our front door. A man yelled something undecipherable. Paw shouted out a few words I wasn't allowed to say and ran to the door, unbolting it, only to find Mr. Derryhill being uncharacteristically frantic.

"Fire! Over there!" he screamed.

Without hesitation, Paw ran out the door and into the storm.

"Stay inside! All of you!" he yelled back through the open door.

Roy Boy and I ran to the window, with Mom following close behind. Through the blackness, we could see orange flames beyond the furthest cabin, reaching high into the night sky. Paw dashed back into the house.

"Blankets and buckets! Fast!

We gathered up the blankets from our beds as quickly as we could. Paw snatched them from us and ran to the edge of the camp. I could barely make out the shapes of Mike, Mr. Bantom and Mr. Derryhill, all running toward the flames with their arms full of blankets. We filled the few buckets we had with our precious rainwater, reserving a little for necessities. I didn't mind if this meant no baths for a while. I saw Paw running toward us. He grabbed the buckets out of our hands, not taking even a second to answer the questions Mom threw at him about the fire.

"Keep filling them buckets as fast as you can when we bring them back!" Paw yelled as he took off with two of them, sloshing part of their contents on the ground as he ran.

Soon, the reserved rainwater was gone, but I knew the creeks would be overflowing with water we could use for everyday purposes. If these storms kept up, which was sometimes the pattern when the weather's been warm, Mom told me, our drinking water supply would quickly be replenished.

On his last trip back down to where we stood, Paw yelled at us to go back in the cabin and stand guard in case the fire got out of hand and spread throughout the camp. We needed to gather up as many things we could save, should our cabin catch fire. I wondered where we would take these things if we had to relocate? Back home?

"Kids, remember, only the things we absolutely need. And, remember also, you each only have two hands to carry stuff with, so don't get carried away," Mom advised.

Roy Boy and I helped her stack food and basic utensils

together next to the cabin's door. My brother and I wanted to go outside and watch, but Mom made us stay inside, out of the storm.

"You don't want to get struck by lightning or hit by fallen limbs, do you?" she asked.

In all the frantic gathering and the fascination with the fire, I had even forgotten about the scary storm raging. With our job done, we dragged dining chairs over and felt helpless as the three of us kept vigil at the cabin window. All we could do was wait and see what damage the morning light would reveal.

Our cabin was spared. As the first bit of sun appeared, Mom, Roy Boy and I ventured outside to see what had happened to the rest of the camp. In the distance, we saw charred trees and smoke rising from a large area behind Mr. Bantom's cabin. The men, soot-covered and weary-looking, shoveled mud over the smoldering ground. The closer we got to where they worked, the more extensive the damage appeared.

"Was it lightning?" Mom called out.

"Yeah. It blew up our gasoline barrel. Would've been worse if we hadn't grounded it. Bad thing is, we ain't got any more fuel for the generator. But I doubt that old thing would still work even if we had gas because it got real charred, too. Pretty bad damage to the back of Bantom's cabin, in fact it's mostly gone. The lean-to was burnt to ashes, too. It's still hot, so you all need to get away and let us work," Paw said.

"Oh, my. That's awful," Mom said under her breath. "I guess Mr. Bantom will have to give up his idea of getting some heat and light to the other cabins."

"Why's that, Mom?" I asked.

"We needed the generator for that," she replied. "It's going to be a cold, dark winter without it."

I didn't like the sound of that comment. I hoped we'd be back at Burnt Willow by the time the weather turned bitter. *Would Santa know where to find us?*

When Mom and I got back to our cabin, she pulled out a set of fresh sheets and laid them on the small sofa.

"Effie, we'll move your cot into the other room so Mr. Bantom can sleep on the sofa. Seems the hospitable thing to do. He'll need a place to bunk while his cabin gets repaired. He can stay out here with Roy Boy."

I felt proud that I'd be sleeping in the room with Mom and Paw while my brother had to stay behind in the living room. I couldn't wait to see his face. This was a special privilege given to us back home when we got sick to our stomachs and needed to be closer to the bathroom. Mom would run Paw out of the bed and tuck us in next to her so she could keep careful watch over us.

I didn't have to wait long before Roy Boy and Timmy came through the front door, followed closely by Tippy.

"'Fraid you're gonna have to sleep out here while I stay in the room with Mom and

Paw. It's a hospital thing."

Roy Boy looked at Mom who giggled and replied, "Hospitable, Effie. That means it's kind and welcoming.

You invite people in when they need a place to stay. I'm going to invite Mr. Bantom to stay with us at night while his cabin is being repaired. The fire burned up the back part of his cabin. Can't have him sleeping there all exposed to the elements," she said as she spread a cover over the couch. "What if it rained? He'd get soaked."

"They chose me to stay in their room. Sorry." I could almost see the wheels turning in my brother's head as he tried to save face in front of Timmy.

"So. Good. Hope you get some sleep listening to Paw's snoring all night. It'll be fun talking to Mr. Bantom about hunting and stuff. Kind of like a sleepover. Boys only."

I stuck my tongue out at him as he walked off with Timmy, who followed behind like a puppy.

"I'd better help Mom get my cot into their room," I stated loudly, just to get that one, last jab in at Roy Boy. He didn't take my bait this time. "Guess I'll get to stay up each night."

Mom had us carry in all the things we piled on the porch last night in our effort to save them from the fire. I was glad we lost nothing, but now everything had to be put back in place quickly in preparation of Mr. Bantom's arrival. By the way Mom was preparing for him, it seemed to be a foregone conclusion he'd agree to bunk with us. I was excited, but I wondered how Paw would feel. The horrible words I'd overheard Paw say the other night were still playing through my head.

CHAPTER FIFTEEN

"Roy, I don't want to put anyone out. Really. I'll be okay sleeping in my cabin. I can put a tarp over the side," Mr. Bantom's voice boomed through the early evening's darkness. Mom held a lantern in one hand, and my hand in her other, as we stood on the front porch of our cabin. I tightened my grasp in excitement as they stepped onto the porch.

"Come on in and make yourself at home. I know you men have had a hard day. Dinner's ready. The other families have already been fed. Mike stopped by and grabbed a little something, but said he was too tired to eat," Mom said, moving out of the way. "Effie, why don't you show Mr. Bantom where he can put his things.

"Don't have many things. Won't be imposing on you very long."

I got the impression he wasn't too happy about staying with us, so I decided it was my mission to make him feel welcome.

"We can play some games later and maybe tell ghost

stories in front of the fireplace." I waited for his answer, but received only a grunt in reply.

"Effie, leave him alone. The men are pretty tired."

"Are you, Mr. Bantom? Tired?"

"That's an understatement. I'm whooped."

Mr. Bantom winked at me and rubbed his sooty face, before flopping his satchel on the floor next to the couch. "Maybe tomorrow. We'll see."

I didn't sense a whole lot of sincerity in his voice, but it gladdened me to think he might be agreeable to playing. Paw hadn't been too much fun the last few weeks.

"I've filled a basin with soapy water if you men want to wash your faces and hands a little before you eat. Your food'll stay hot while you do that," Mom said, stirring the pot over the fire.

"I ain't worried about the food being hot," Mr. Bantom laughed. "I think I could heat it up just standing near it. Actually, eating it cold sounds pretty good to me. Working near them embers all day has a way of making a body hot and sweaty!"

"I suppose that's true. Too bad we don't have a milk cow or I could've churned some ice cream." She set plates on the table and poured water in the cups I put out earlier. "We'll need one more cup, Effie. Will you please get one for me? Kids, you go ahead and eat so the men can have their dinner in peace when they're ready."

Mom served my plate and handed it to me. Chicken stew again. Roy Boy grabbed his plate and hovered over Mom, making sure she gave him enough.

"I want that piece right there," he said, pointing to a large piece of chicken in the pot.

"We need to save some meat for the men. They've worked up quite an appetite, I'm sure." Mom chopped a tiny piece off the chunk of chicken, set it on Roy Boy's plate and smiled. She never could resist his requests. "But no seconds tonight."

I had noticed that our portions of food were getting smaller and smaller with each meal served. Mom told me we had to be careful with our rations if we wanted them to last through the winter. Winter was still a couple of months away, so I wondered if we'd all starve by then. Every day, I counted the jars in the closet to see how many were left. Tomatoes were fine. Carrots were a little slim, but that's okay, I don't like them. The meat jars definitely were disappearing. We'd dipped the eggs in wax to make them last longer and laid them carefully in a basket at the bottom of the pantry closet. Seemed to be a pretty good supply of them around. And I saw a couple of buckets under the kitchen table, so Mom still had some wheatberries to grind for bread.

Paw and Mr. Bantom huddled over the basin in the corner of the cabin. "After you," Bantom said to Paw who had already started rinsing. Water ran off his arms in sooty streams. Paw grabbed the rag Ma handed him and must not have done a very good job cleaning up because the rag was covered in gray smears when he finished drying his hands. He draped it on the back of a wooden dining chair while Mr. Bantom took his turn splashing his face with the sudsy water. Upon the second large splash to his face, he grabbed the grubby rag and held it to his eyes and proceeded to scream things I'd never heard before. By the look on Mom's face, I knew the things he said violated Paw's rule about cussing. Mr. Bantom vigorously rubbed his eyes.

"That lye soap in there?!" Bantom bellowed. "Get me some dab-gum water – fast!" He snatched the large glass of water Mom handed him. He opened his eyes squinty-like and ran to the front door. I can only assume he threw the water into his eye because when he came back inside, the entire front of his shirt was soaked.

"Sorry about the fit I pitched. That's mighty powerful soap in that water."

Mom was silent. She nodded her forgiveness but looked as if she'd received a lashing with a belt.

Paw, with a grin on his face, didn't seem too terribly upset.

"Maybe oughta use some of that soap on your mouth, Bantom!" He bent over in hysterics, which I just didn't understand because I would've gotten a major whooping if I had so much as said the four-letter-word where the devil lives. A shocked expression remained on Roy Boy's face telling me he'd probably never heard those words before - - at least not from someone he knew and respected. I, on the other hand, had eavesdropped on enough conversations between Mr. Bantom and Paw to know he was no saint.

"Wow," I whispered to him. "I t-nac eveileb motnab dias dab words." I watched Roy Boy toss around in his head what I said until a look of knowing flashed across his face.

"Wap oughta teg, um . . . his tleb out, um, retfa him." He grinned, and if I didn't know better, I believe he actually enjoyed our little secret code talk. He'd always made fun of me in the past because he couldn't figure out what I was saying. We giggled, and in that moment, I felt a friendly bond with my older brother. He'd learn the satisfaction of venting in a language no one else understood.

Mr. Bantom sat at my vacated spot at the table and wrapped his arm around the bowl of stew looking like a wild mother animal protecting her young. Paw took his place across from him and tucked his napkin into his shirt. I watched the stew dribble off of Bantom's spoon and run down his chin. He lifted his arm and wiped. I could hear each swallow gurgle its way down his throat. He slopped up the stew, belched and slammed his spoon down on the table. Did he even chew his food? I was glad I'd already eaten. I probably would've thrown up if I had to sit with him at the table and try to eat. Paw seemed sophisticated in comparison. Paw looked up from his dinner and must've noticed my gaping mouth.

"What're you lookin' at?" He growled.

"Nothing. Just wondering if you need anything else. More water?" I glanced at Roy Boy, who let out a sigh. "Musta been good stew, huh?" I said, giving Roy Boy one more look to reassure him that I had the situation under control. Maybe I shouldn't be so proud of my ability to bluff my way out of trouble . . . but I was.

"Why don't you young 'uns go get ready for bed? It's been a hard day, and I'm ready for some sleep. Don't want you all keepin' me up with your chatter," Paw said. "Lights are going out in thirty minutes. Lulu, you need to get in bed first, and try to fall asleep so you don't wake me up wigglin' around on your cot. Go ahead and get your Bear Bear or whatever you need and put it in the room."

What? I thought I'd get to stay up late because I was sleeping in the gown-ups' room.

I avoided looking at Roy Boy, who I was sure felt

vindicated after I ribbed him about being banished from the bedroom.

"Sure. I'm pretty bushed," I lied.

I lay on my cot trying my hardest to feign sleep as Paw and Mom crawled under the covers in their bed. Within a few minutes, Paw's snoring began. I couldn't believe how loud it sounded being in the same room with him. *How does Mom put up with that night after night?* I counted snores. I pretended the snores were a grizzly bear's growling like I'd seen on TV shows back home. I put my fingers in my ears in a failed effort to drown out the noise. I thought about getting up and moving into the other room with Roy Boy and Mr. Bantom, but knew I'd have to explain. The only thing I could do was suffer and try to fall asleep, which I must've done eventually because the next thing I heard was the sound of Mom opening the door to go start breakfast. Upon raising my head a little, I could see Paw still asleep in the bed. This gave me an excuse to try and make up some of the sleep I lost earlier in the evening. His snoring had now subsided. How wonderful my warm covers felt as I pulled them higher around my neck and allowed my thoughts to turn to my precious Tippy, who sneaked into the room when Mom went out. Tippy curled up next to my cot. I lowered my arm out of the covers and draped it over the dog until I fell asleep.

— • ● • —

Paw and the other men began work on Mr. Bantom's

cabin as soon as the sun rose and planned to stay at it until darkness overtook the light. Roy Boy and I crept to the other side of camp to watch, off and on, for most of the early day. Timmy joined us whenever he could escape the ever-watchful eyes of his mother. We had to be stealthy while there because Paw didn't like kids disrupting work with silly questions. One more word from us, and I believe Paw would've banished us from ever coming back to watch. We were fascinated with the charred remains of the cabin. This was the first burned-down house we'd ever seen in person. The remains of the blackened back wall had been torn out and lay in a heap beside the left side of the structure which had not been damaged quite as badly. Peering into the open end of the cabin, we could see the front door dead ahead of us. Timmy told us it was like looking into a movie set. We figured he knew what he was talking about since his family took a movie studio tour on their trip to Los Angeles the previous year.

Mr. Mike noticed us nosing around. At first, we thought we'd be sent away immediately, but he then began explaining to us that the large posts on the end of the cabin were to keep the roof from falling in. He warned us not to enter the cabin for fear of a collapse. I had to giggle a little, standing at the opening of the cabin, surrounded by smoke-laden air. For a moment, I felt as if I were a tiny person, standing in the fireplace back at the cabin.

Roy Boy, Timmy, and I soon became bored, so we headed to the main cabin knowing Mom would be preparing lunch.

"Why don't Mr. Bantom move into Mr. Chris' old cabin?" I asked her.

"I suppose it's because they never finished the walls before Mr. Chris left, so I imagine it gets pretty chilly at night in there. That tarp doesn't insulate very much. We have a nice warm place to offer him, so it's the Christian thing to do. The nights are starting to get cool, and his sleeping bag isn't gonna be snug enough in another few weeks, I assume." Mom paused for a moment, then began wiping off the kitchen table as she continued her thought. "In fact, Mr. Bantom owns this cabin, so he needs no invitation. He's been kind to let us live here."

"Oh," I replied. I'd forgotten about that. "You don't think he'll make us leave, do you?"

"Absolutely not. Mr. Bantom's a generous man and would never think of putting us out in the cold."

"But he could, couldn't he?" I began scratching my arms.

"Put that thought out of your mind, Effie. It won't ever happen. Your Paw and Mr. Bantom are friends, and have been for a long, long time. Their friendship is important to 'em. That's what friends do for each other. I'm sure you'd do the same for Timmy, right?"

I thought about that for a second but didn't answer. I didn't want to hurt Timmy's feelings.

"I think Mr. Bantom has always thought of himself as an uncle to you kids. When you were missing, it was like his own kin was lost. You should've seen how worried he was. I don't know what we would've done without his help, not to mention how he calmed your Paw down."

Mom handed each of us a sandwich wrapped in a napkin. "Now go and take these to the men, then come right back and get your own to eat."

I handed the sandwich I'd been holding to Roy Boy, deciding I'd rather wait inside with Mom. Mrs. Derryhill and Michelle entered the cabin and began setting the table and filling cups of water for the women and children.

"I'm afraid we're having the same old thing today. Peanut butter." This had become Mom's mantra every time anyone came in for lunch over the past couple of weeks.

"No need to apologize," Michelle answered. "We should be grateful for anything we get." I noticed Mrs. Derryhill cast her eyes downward. She said nothing. Her silence told me that gratitude may not have been what she felt.

"Do we have any of those biscuits left from breakfast, Vinca?" Mrs. Derryhill asked. "I might like to put my peanut butter on one of those, if you don't mind. And maybe some jelly, if you have a jar open."

"We need to be careful about using up our supplies before winter times come around. Oh, go ahead and pick one out from the pantry. We'll open it," Mom said. "I'm sorry. I shouldn't have said that in a snappy way. I'm just thinking that when winter comes, jelly may be the only treat we have to look forward to."

I went over to the pantry and looked inside before Mrs. Derryhill got there. Only ten jars of jam and jelly remained on the shelves. We'd already used up most of our supply. I moved out of the way to let Mrs. Derryhill pick out the one she wanted. Behind her back, I turned and gave Mom a distressed look. Mom raised her finger to her mouth. After Mrs. Derryhill left the pantry doorway, I went back over and counted all the jars of food. Eight jars of various meat from animals Paw and Mr. Bantom had shot — I didn't want to ask what; ten tomatoes; six carrots; three green beans; twelve more jars of assorted things such as soup and relishes. Throughout the summer, the jars of meat and vegetables were barely touched because our garden was going strong and, of course, we always had eggs from our chickens. Paw had been able to buy a couple more chickens from his source earlier in the summer. We ate a few of them. The remaining chickens were still laying, but the cooler weather seemed to be causing that to wane a little. Mom had us put extra straw in their pen and we wrapped a tarp around one side to keep some of the cold wind off them. She said it was important they had plenty of light and water. We tossed dried ears of corn into the sunny corner of the pen to keep them in the light as much as possible. They enjoyed pecking at these.

I watched carefully and bit my tongue as Mrs. Derryhill carried the blueberry jam to the table. That was my favorite, and the last one of its kind. She pried the jar open and plopped a heaping glob onto a biscuit, licked the spoon and paused. She must've thought no one was looking because she dipped the spoon back into the jar and shoved a spoonful into her mouth. She turned toward me and, by the look on her face, realized she'd been caught in her disgusting act. I wondered how many times in the past she'd done this, which caused me to cringe.

"Close your mouth. The flies are bad today," Mrs. Derryhill said to me under her breath. I wasn't sure if she was kidding or just showing a mean-spirited side.

I shut my gaping mouth and wanted to cry right there in front of her. She'd contaminated a perfectly good jar of blueberry jam, and I was the only one who witnessed it. I would've expected my brother to do something like that, but not a grown-up woman. Mom would tell me to stop being a tattletale, I was sure, if I disclosed what I saw Mrs. Derryhill do. So, I quietly seethed as I took a bite from my peanut butter sandwich. Boy would blueberry jam have tasted good on it, if only . . .

CHAPTER SIXTEEN

Over the next few weeks, what started off as a fun adventure of having Mr. Bantom staying with us, lost its appeal as I sensed a growing tension between Paw and him. Bad weather caused the repair to Mr. Bantom's cabin to drag on and on, and I knew Mr. Bantom would rather be sleeping out under the trees than here with two restless kids and a best friend who spoke harshly to him. I heard him express this thought to the others when Paw walked away to go to the outhouse one afternoon.

Paw withdrew from us, for the most part, and because we were trapped inside for many days waiting for the cold rain to stop, we often turned to Mr. Bantom to play games with us. I hoped that Paw would get jealous seeing us interact with him, but he didn't even seem to notice. Mr. Bantom, on the other hand, noticed. He began excusing himself to the porch every time Roy Boy, Timmy, or I mentioned playing tic tac toe, tag, or hide and seek. I suppose about fifty times of being named "safe" when we played tag wore him down a little.

"Come on, kids," he'd say. "Go ask your Paw to play with you for a while."

"But Paw told us not to bug him," I'd say back.

"Your Paw's a smart man," he'd reply. "Smart enough to disappear at the right time."

I think Mom was feeling ignored by Paw too. She spent many evenings sitting by herself next to the fire with a book in her hands. Every now and then, I'd catch her glancing over at the bedroom doorway as if waiting for Paw to walk through to where we all gathered. Sometimes, if Mr. Bantom went outside to sit on the porch or take a walk, Paw would come into the room and ask Mom to make him a cup of tea. He said it soothed his nerves. This, in itself, was unusual. Until a few weeks ago, Paw never had a taste for tea and said it was only for girls. He once declared, when Mom asked him if he'd like a cup, "When you see me wearing a skirt and frilly hat, you'll know I'm ready for a tea party. So, no point in asking me until then."

At the time he said that, I thought it was funny, but soon realized he was being dead serious. His recent change in taste took us all by surprise, and I'll have to admit that I can't get the picture of Paw in a skirt and frilly hat out of my head each time he sits at the table sipping a cup of chamomile tea. But Paw wasn't asking for a cup tonight. He didn't walk through the doorway at all.

"Mom?" I whispered in her ear. "What's the matter with Paw?"

She sat in silence for a moment before answering. "I wish I knew, honey. I wish I knew. Sometimes men just have a lot of things on their minds, like how to take care of their families and such. Just give him a little time. Living out here has been a big adjustment for us all."

"How much time? I miss him."

"I figure he probably misses us, too, Honey, so it won't be long 'til he gets things figured out."

I hoped she was right and was determined to speed things along any way I could. Roy Boy busied himself with a stick he was carving on while Timmy played with the wood shavings. I tip-toed into the bedroom to where Paw stood. When I wrapped my arms around him, he startled to my touch.

"Sorry, Paw. I felt like you might need a hug."

He turned to me, his eyes looked sunken. His face was expressionless. Paw rubbed my hair, like he used to do when I was younger, then clung to me. His chest heaved as he sobbed quietly.

"It'll be okay, Paw. You'll get things figured out real soon," was all I could think of saying. I'd only seen Paw cry once before. He wept bitterly as he stood by my grandfather's casket the day of his funeral. Although I was barely walking at the time, it left me with a memory so vivid, I'll carry it with me the rest of my life. That was the night I saw Knock for the second time. He was behind Paw, watching him but not saying a word. Knock came to me and laid his hand on my shoulder as if to comfort me, then he was gone.

"Can I get you some tea?" I asked him quietly.

He nodded his head slowly and replied in a voice barely above a whisper, "That would be nice, Lulu."

When I walked back into the other room, all eyes were on me. Mom started to get up as I neared the pot of hot water, but I threw my arm out to her in a gesture showing I had things under control. She watched me carefully as I filled the tea ball with chamomile leaves, then poured the scalding water into a mug. I plopped the ball into the water, splashing a little onto my arm. Boy, did it hurt, but I pretended not to notice. When the water turned the appropriate color, I spooned some sugar in, stirred, and carried it into the bedroom where Paw now sat on the bed.

Paw took the mug from me and rubbed my head one more time. He patted me on the back, winked and gently shooshed me toward the door.

"He's just figuring things, I suppose," I bent and whispered to Mom. "He'll be okay."

Mom pulled me to her and held me tight.

"You're a tender soul, Effie Dee," she said, kissing me on the cheek. "God has given you an extra dose of sweetness."

I felt proud. Proud and sad. I helped Mom clear away the dinner dishes, then dried as she handed me each washed, dripping plate. I thought staying busy would keep my mind off Paw, but I was wrong. The thought of him holding me tightly while sobbing haunted the remainder of the evening.

Eventually, Paw emerged from the bedroom acting as if nothing was going on with him. He shot a glance at me, smiled, and went to take his place at the vacant dinner table. Mom had saved a plate of food for him, should he develop an appetite, so I ran to the kitchen counter and retrieved it for him.

"I'm glad you decided to eat, Paw. You need to keep your strength up," I said, setting it down in front of him. "It was real good. Has some onion in it tonight." We had gotten used to the stew Mom made from whatever she could forage, mixed with a skimpy helping of a canned vegetable from our summer garden. We alternated between stew and "forage porridge", as Mom would call it. There remained in the garden some root vegetables and a potato here and there. We left them underground thinking it might preserve them a bit longer. Mom said we would soon dig up the few remaining potatoes, beets and carrots because the cold weather would be here to stay before long. I looked forward to working with Mom in the garden. To me, it was a miracle to see a vegetable emerge from the ground, or to cut one from a plant. I decided I'd make a good farmer someday.

Mr. Bantom sat on the front porch for a couple of hours. I was sure he was waiting for us all to go to bed so he could have some peace and quiet. He must've been freezing because there had been a drop in temperature since yesterday and rain fell steadily and hard. I figured we kids had gotten under his skin badly for him to endure the raw weather just to avoid us.

As Mom tucked me into bed for the night, Mr. Bantom came inside the cabin with Mr. Mike. My door was propped open, so I heard the panic in Mr. Mike's voice.

"I think the baby's coming," he said, breathlessly. "I need Vinca to come quickly," he told Paw.

Mom left the bedroom and went to see what was happening. "How far apart are her pains?" she asked Mr. Mike.

"I don't know. But she's hurting real bad and asked me to get you to come."

"Go back to her and I'll pack up a few things and see you in a couple of minutes. Try to keep her calm," Mom said.

Mr. Mike ran out of the cabin, leaving Mom to scurry around, gathering things from the pantry. I whispered a prayer for Mrs. Michelle and the baby, then tried hard to fall asleep. I heard Paw tell Roy Boy goodnight then walk out onto the porch. Curiosity got the best of me, so I crept into the living room and sat on a stool near the front door, listening intently to things I later wished I hadn't heard.

"How long are you going to keep this charade going, Roy?" Mr. Bantom said to Roy Sr. "You gonna wait until we all freeze to death? Or maybe we'll starve first."

"The President's getting ready to meet with Congress about the oil crisis. Something big's gettin' ready to happen soon. The radio reporter said this could be the end of our freedom. People are already riotin' and can't get gas to fill their car tanks."

"Don't know what kind of crazy programs you're listening to, but you know there ain't no oil crisis, Roy. Just let us all go back, and we'll take our chances," Mr. Bantom said, loudly thumping his fingers on the arm of the rocking chair. "This is just plain crazy."

"You're not going back, Bantom. So don't even think about trying. You'll have a target on your back if you attempt to leave camp. I don't want to see you hurt."

"Is that a threat, Roy? I know you don't want Vinca to know that you risked the garage, but is that really worth hurting a friend? We've known each other a long time."

"It's not a threat, Bantom. It's a reality. You ain't going back. I won't let you leave and get us all in trouble. Friend or no friend, I can't let you leave," Paw said.

"I'm going to bed," Mr. Bantom declared as he rose from the chair. "Good night. Go do the same, Roy."

I dashed back to my bedroom, barely making it through the doorway before Mr. Banton quietly entered.

Paw remained on the porch for several minutes before coming inside, where it was warm. I peeked from the dark doorway to make sure Paw didn't do anything crazy. A fire still burned in the large fireplace, and I could see in the dim glow that Roy Boy was sound asleep on his cot in the living room. Mr. Bantom took off his shoes and crawled into his makeshift bed as Paw passed through the room and grabbed his rifle from its place in the corner. Without a word being exchanged, Paw walked toward where I stood. He didn't spot me because his gaze remained fixed on Mr. Bantom, as he lay on the couch. I jumped onto my cot and buried myself completely under the covers. Paw must've believed I was asleep. I listened for noises of him crawling into his bed, but heard none, so I wiggled a little and made some yawning sounds, drawing the covers slowly down so I could see what was happening. I quickly closed my eyes and acted as though I'd fallen back asleep.

Paw sat on the corner of the bed for a moment, then rose and quietly walked to the side window. He stood and looked toward the cabin where his wife tended the laboring Michelle.

He pushed his face closer in order to see better. I had watched from that same window earlier, before Paw and Mr. Bantom fussed on the porch, so I knew you could see a faint lantern's glow coming through the window of that cabin.

"Bantom ain't gonna rob me of anything that ain't rightfully his. It's over my dead body he'll take my garage away from me. I've gotta take care of my family," he whispered, then wiped his foggy breath from the window, using the palm of his hand.

He propped the rifle against the bedroom wall and slipped under the cool covers of his bed, pulling the blanket up around his neck to keep the draft away. I stirred a little in my cot before finally being able to settle into sleep.

It was late in the morning before Mom returned to our cabin. She flopped onto a chair in the living room, pushed the hair out of her face and sighed.

"What a long night," she exclaimed. "But we have a girl! She's very tiny and came a little early, so we'll need to watch her carefully."

I was excited about the thought of another girl living at camp. Roy Boy slapped his forehead with his open hand and dropped his head to his chest.

"Oh brother," he said. "Just what we need."

"My thoughts exactly. A squawking baby screaming all night. At least it won't be under our roof," Paw said. "Better their problem than ours."

Mom sat quietly and closed her eyes before speaking. "It's mighty chilly in their cabin. No fireplace to keep that new baby warm. Babies need to stay warm, especially premature ones."

"What are you gettin' at, Vinca? Michelle will keep that baby warm."

"Michelle isn't going to be holding her daughter

twenty-four hours a day. She has to put her down at some point. Did you know that they have breezes blowing in through the gaps in their wall?"

"It ain't my fault they decided to reproduce. And don't go gettin' any crazy thoughts," Paw warned. "I ain't runnin' no hotel, and I especially ain't runnin' no daycare."

I noticed that Mom had fallen asleep sitting up, so I went to her and propped a pillow behind her head. She roused a little, patted me on the hand and fell back into a sound sleep.

Mr. Bantom, who had been listening to the entire conversation, got up from his seat and walked outside. We didn't see him again until dinner time, but I suspect the news was just too much for him to take. Paw sat on the porch until his return, his rifle by his side. I could tell there would be some lively discussions around the dinner table that night, and my suspicions were correct.

CHAPTER SEVENTEEN

Michelle and the baby arrived at our cabin the following morning bright and early. I had never seen a newborn baby before and was fascinated at the tiny, wrinkled thing wrapped tightly, making sucking motions with her tiny, blistered lips.

"Can I hold her?" I had to restrain my urge to pull her out of her mother's arms.

Michelle looked at Mom who immediately answered for her. "Effie, you're too young to hold a newborn. Maybe when she's a little older Mrs. Michelle will let you hold her in your lap."

Tippy jumped up from the floor each time the baby squealed. He sniffed at the bottom of the bundle Michelle held as she sat in the rocking chair by the fire.

"Have you decided on a name yet?" Mom asked.

"We're thinking about naming her Josie after my grandmother. Mike isn't completely convinced, but we had a deal that if I had a girl, I got to choose the name. If we had a boy, he would've named him."

"I think that's a fine name for a little girl. I like it a lot," Mom said. I nodded my approval and went about playing with my paper dolls I'd fashioned from pieces of cardboard.

The rain and wind had finally come to an end allowing us to escape our small space, which was beginning to get crowded. Paw, Mr. Banton, Mr. Derryhill and Mr. Mike went about work on the burnt cabin. I'd take a break from my playing every hour or so to check on the men's progress. Now that Michelle and the baby were staying with us, I found myself wishing that Mr. Bantom could go home. His constant bickering with Paw was getting on my nerves.

From a distance, I could tell the men were having to slop around in mud as they worked on repairing the back wall and roof. The tarp they had thrown over the top of the cabin's roof must've blown off in the rainstorms. I saw it lying crumpled in the middle of the field where our summer garden used to be.

I walked back into the cabin in time to hear the baby start crying. Michelle rose and went into the bedroom, closed the door, and nursed her away from our curious eyes. Roy Boy decided to go to the Derryhill's place to play with Timmy. Mom suggested that she and I go dig up the remaining vegetables from the garden while the earth was soft from the rain. I eagerly ran to the porch to grab the shovel and waited for her to catch up.

"Go change into your gardening shoes, Effie. The mud will be knee-high to an elephant, I suppose, and it's too cold to go barefooted. So don't even ask."

We carried a box to the garden and dug where some plant tops remained above the ground, now covered in mud. Soon, the box had a small collection of beets, carrots and a few potatoes. I was especially proud when I found an onion hidden in the soil. A couple of turnips were hiding at the far end of the garden. We'd eaten the greens and hoped the turnips would stay fresh underground until time to finish our harvesting.

"We'll leave these in the metal box on our porch," Mom explained. It should be about the right temperature to keep them from spoilin' until we use them. Like an outdoor refrigerator. And if it gets below freezing, most of these should be okay. We can take the potatoes and the onion inside, I suppose," she said, stacking our produce into the box. "This isn't going to last us long, but I'm thankful for every bit of it. Let's go inside and get the mud washed off."

Michelle was back in the living room rocking the baby when we entered the cabin. "Josie's just about to fall asleep," she said, smiling at the tiny hairless baby.

"So, you decided on her name?" Mom asked.

"I couldn't keep calling her 'the baby' could I now? Much nicer to call her by name."

"Mom? Where's Michelle going to sleep?"

"We'll work out something."

"I'll sleep on the floor by the fire. Michelle can have my cot."

"That's nice of you Effie. I was thinking that maybe the girls will all stay in the bedroom and the boys can stay in the living room. I'll ask your Paw what he thinks about that plan."

"Where's Mr. Mike going to be?" I asked.

Michelle responded in a low voice, not wishing to wake the sleeping baby. "Mr. Mike will be okay in the cabin. He has a warm sleeping bag. He'll come down and be with us until bedtime each night."

Mom cut up some of the vegetables we harvested, added them to a broth she prepared, turning it into a soup for dinner. She thickened it with flour to make it more filling, she said, then set it far in the back of the fireplace to keep it warm. Everyone expected hot food now that colder weather had arrived. No longer did they elect to take food items to their individual cabins to eat or sit at the picnic table in front of our cabin as they did during the summer months. Mom was preparing the dinners most evenings and since we were the only ones with a fireplace, the families ate around our big table in shifts.

One by one, the men came to the cabin and washed at the large, galvanized basin by the dining area wall. First, the men were served dinner, followed by Michelle and the kids. Finally, Mom and Mrs. Derryhill ate their soup then cleared away all the dishes. Everyone lingered longer than usual. I suspected they were just as stir-crazy as my family and tired of looking at their own four walls. I pulled out games, hoping someone would take the bait. Only the children thought it was a good idea, so we found a clear space on the cabin floor and laid out the Monopoly board. None of us really knew the official rules, so we improvised best we could. As usual, we grew weary of trying to buy real estate and began playing "store" with the phony money. I took things from around the cabin and set them on the kitchen counter, assuming the position of storekeeper, which infuriated Roy Boy. Timmy wisely defused the impending argument by suggesting that he and Roy Boy rob my store and tie me up. Game over. I was impressed with Timmy's manipulative skills, but a little disturbed they took such a violent bent. I went back to my paper dolls and left them to play however they wished.

Baby Josie's screaming gave me an excuse to go see what was going on. "What's wrong with her?" I asked Michelle, who was holding the baby on her shoulder, patting her gently.

"Not sure. I just fed her, so she can't be hungry. Don't think she's wet either." She continued patting Josie as Mom walked to where they were.

"Here, let me take her and give you a little break." Michelle handed the baby to Mom, but the wailing continued.

"Oh, Josie. Don't fuss, honey." Mom walked around the cabin holding the baby. Mr. Mike bent down to the baby and stroked her cheek lightly. I noticed that Mr. Bantom and Paw were nowhere to be seen. Neither said anything before leaving, but both had disgruntled looks on their faces earlier in the evening. Every time baby Josie cried, they looked at each other and shook their heads. I thought I heard Mr. Bantom say a bad word, but it was difficult to tell because the crying drowned out all conversation that wasn't at an elevated pitch.

"She sure has strong lungs," Mrs. Derryhill said, trying to look pleasant. Her smile didn't seem genuine to me. "Where'd you get diapers?" she asked.

"Vinca was nice enough to cut up some soft clothes and stitch them together."

I noticed that the baby had one of Paw's bandanas around her behind, keeping the cloth diaper from falling off. I was surprised Paw didn't say anything about it when he was in the room. Maybe he hadn't seen it yet.

"I have a Bear Bear she can play with," I offered. "Let me go get him." I dashed out of the room and grabbed the doll off the cot in the bedroom and handed it to Michelle. Michelle took my offering and thanked me for my thoughtfulness. Before she could get it away from the baby, Josie popped the doll's ear into her mouth.

"Effie, baby Josie might be too young to play with that for a while, but that was very sweet of you," Mom said, taking the grubby little doll from Michelle's outstretched hand. "Maybe we should wash Bear Bear, and Josie can play with him in a few months."

I held Bear Bear by its dry ear and carried it back to the bedroom, wiping off his wet ear on the bedspread.

"I'm sorry Bear Bear. I didn't know Josie would slobber on you." I sniffed the doll's head and set it on the end of the cot to dry completely. I think Tippy must've gotten ahold of Bear Bear again by the smell of the doll's fur. The fragrance of soured, wet dog.

I went back into the room where everyone was congregated. Mrs. Derryhill had a distasteful expression on her face as she whined to Mom about how cold their cabin is.

"You can stand by the windows and feel a cold breeze blowing in," she said. "Isn't there anything we can do about this. I just don't know how much longer I can take it."

"I'm sorry. You know you're welcome to come sit by the fire anytime you want. This cabin belongs to everyone here," Mom graciously answered.

"I have already put four blankets on Timmy at night. Poor thing. He had to wear his knit cap on his head last night. He'll freeze to death if it gets any colder."

"Mom, I'm really not all that ——"

"Timmy," Mrs. Derryhill interrupted, "You were shaking when I tucked you in last night." Timmy looked at me and Roy Boy and shrugged. He silently mouthed at us that he really wasn't that cold at all. "I just don't understand how come your family gets to stay in the warm cabin while the rest of us are in the cold."

"I'm really sorry you feel that way," Mom replied. "We explained to everyone the situation when we moved up here. I don't mind cooking for everyone and sharing our cabin with anyone who would like to be here with us." I could tell the hurtful remarks upset Mom. Her neck turned blotchy, and she cast her eyes downward briefly, not making eye contact with Mrs. Derryhill.

"Well, we just might take you up on that. We'd better get back to the arctic now. It's getting late. Good night, all." Mrs. Derryhill motioned to Timmy; her husband had already left the gathering after he ate his dinner.

After they departed, I turned to Mom and said, "Can't Timmy stay here with us? He can have my cot. I don't want him freezing to death."

"Timmy's not gonna freeze to death, honey. Some people just like to complain," Mom said. "I'm sorry. I'm a Christian woman and shouldn't have said that to you. I guess we're all a little tense lately."

When Paw and Mr. Bantom got back to the cabin, Paw looked around and commented, "Getting a little late isn't it?" He stared dead at Michelle and the baby.

"Roy, Michelle will be sleeping in the bedroom with the baby. Effie and I will be in there with her. We figured the men could stay out here together."

"Really? You figure that, huh?" He turned his back to everyone and stood still for a moment before composing himself and facing us again. "Whatever you say. Why don't you go on to bed. I hope I don't hear that baby squawking at all hours of the night. I need some sleep."

Michelle looked as if she wanted to cry. She turned to Mom, pleading to her with her eyes. "What should I do, Vinca? I don't want him to be mad at me."

"You're gonna stay right here, Michelle. You and the baby. Let me handle Roy. He can go stay with Mike if he can't take it. Please don't argue with me, because I'm not going to let you and Josie stay in that cold cabin."

I was excited about having the baby in the cabin with us, but wondered if Mom realized that our cabin, too, had been getting very cold at night when the fire died down. Since men were now sleeping in the living area, they were charged with the task of keeping logs burning throughout the night, but often slept straight on until morning. Mr. Bantom took it upon himself to get up before the rest of us and start the fire up again from the embers that remained.

Right after breakfast, the men continued working on Mr. Bantom's cabin. Mom and Michelle washed Josie's homemade diapers in the galvanized tub and hung them in front of the fire to dry. We had three rows of clothesline strung up across the room, each had six diapers spread out on it in the center where the heat was most concentrated. I noticed that some of the diapers were made from clothing I'd seen Mom wear before. She had cut up a few of her favorite flannel shirts and nightgowns for the cause of providing the baby's needs. I was proud of her unselfish act.

Mom led Michelle to the pantry, pulled out some

canisters, then said, "I'm going to show you how to make a salve for Josie's little behind out of these herbs and oil."

"Now this one has antibacterial properties," she explained, tapping the container of calendula. "These also help that way," she said, setting aside the canisters of marshmallow root and dried elderberries. "What I'm going to do is infuse these herbs into this oil. I'll show you how that's done. Then you'll have a nice protective barrier for Josie's little rear end." Mom began heating the oil over the fire. I couldn't see exactly how she was doing it because the diapers were in the way, so I decided to crash the game of war Roy Boy and Timmy were playing.

Josie started screaming, so Michelle took her into the bedroom to check her diaper. Maybe it was my imagination, but Josie's crying seemed louder than ever. I peeked my head in and the smell overwhelmed me. *How could something that small stink so badly?* Michelle tossed the dirty diaper in a bucket next to the bed and proceeded to clean the baby with a rag.

I went back to the game of war with the boys, just in time to hear them cry out in disgust over the odor of poop, which had now wafted into the rest of the cabin.

"Come on, troops. Let's march outside," Roy Boy commanded.

Sounded like a great idea to me, so I headed out the door behind my "General", only to run back inside quickly to grab my jacket. I held my nose until I was out in the fresh air again. We played in the clearing until time for dinner, then headed in to get cleaned up and set the table. Paw and the other men looked exhausted as they walked through the cabin door. I'll never forget the look of shock on Paw's face as he saw the diapers hanging from the clotheslines.

He violated one of his own rules when he opened his mouth to speak. I'd never heard those words come out of him before. We all stood still and silent. Only the crackle of the fire made a noise. Paw turned and headed out, slamming the cabin door behind him. The other three men were speechless, and I'm not sure if it was because of Paw's rantings or because of the diapers hanging to dry in front of the fire.

"Not a pretty sight to greet you when you walk in, I gotta say," Mr. Bantom said, breaking the silence. "Guess it was more than he could handle."

"Shall we go ahead and eat?" Mr. Derryhill asked.

Mom motioned toward the table, still looking stunned by Paw's outburst. A large pot of hot porridge sat in the middle, with bowls stacked alongside. Mr. Derryhill sat, with Mike and Mr. Bantom following his lead. It was Timmy's turn to say grace, so he stood at the head of the table and bowed his head.

"Dear God. Thank you for this food and please make Mr. Whitley nice again. Amen."

Timmy's father looked a little embarrassed and glanced over at Mom, who resumed the task of pulling diapers off the clotheslines. Michelle rocked Josie in her arms to keep her from crying, I would assume. Just as Mom finished putting the last diaper in the clothes basket, Mrs. Derryhill walked through the cabin door carrying a large suitcase. She set the suitcase on the floor next to the wall.

"Whew!" was all she said. Noticing that all eyes were fixed on her, she then returned the stares. "What're you glaring at?" I quickly turned my head away from her direction. The sharp tone of her voice frightened me.

"Going somewhere?" her husband asked.

"Nope. Not now, because I've gotten where I was going."

I looked at Mom, then to Timmy and Roy Boy. All had expressions of confusion on their faces and remained silent, our stares shifted back toward Mrs. Derryhill for an explanation.

"Why should I be the only one freezing to death? Timmy, I brought you some clothes, too. We're staying here where it's warm. Your Dad may join us, too, if he likes."

Mrs. Derryhill walked to the woodburning stove and poured hot water into a mug. She filled a tea ball with leaves and dipped it into the water to steep. Not a word was spoken back to her, so I gathered we had acquired another houseguest.

CHAPTER EIGHTEEN

Paw didn't return that night. I peeked outside when the sun was coming up and saw him pacing back and forth in front of the cabin Mr. Chris once used. To say that last night was long would be an understatement. The ladies slept, or at least tried to sleep, in the bedroom while the men stayed in the living room stoking the fire throughout the night. Baby Josie only woke two times, which is better than the three times we were told to expect. I felt a bit of relief when Mom rose from bed and began getting herself ready for the day. I was more than ready to go with her into the other room to get breakfast started in order to escape the stench from the diaper pail, which was almost unbearable. Michelle remained on the cot with her arm over the baby who slept on top of her chest. Mrs. Derryhill wiggled around on a make-shift bed she fashioned out of blankets from her cottage and three pillows. Remembering the huge pile of luggage and boxes her family brought with them to the camp, I wondered why she hadn't packed an air mattress in one of them. With all the useless things they did bring, it amazed me they failed to bring some practical items. But I suppose they figured we'd be back in Burnt Willow by now as I, too, had assumed.

In the living room, the men rolled up their sleeping bags to make room for us to walk. Roy Boy and Timmy were sound asleep. Tippy was pacing around like he wanted to go outside and do his business. I couldn't help but feel a little envious that they didn't have to suffer the night with the loud baby and smell of poop. I noticed that Mr. Derryhill was absent and wondered if he went back to his colder cabin to avoid the mounting tension in ours. He struck me as a peace-loving man, and I'd heard Mom once comment that Mrs. Derryhill probably made him step in time to her beat — whatever that meant. Maybe he enjoyed having his cabin to himself.

Mom was unusually quiet as she prepared the oatmeal and heated the kettle of water over the fire. I caught her yawning a few times and rubbing her eyes with the sleeve of her heavy sweater. Mr. Bantom went to the small barrel of water and attempted to wash his face, only to lift a second handful of water to his nose and sniff.

"What the—", he stopped himself and looked at Mom.

I answered for her. "Mrs. Michelle rinsed the baby's diapers out last night." I immediately realized that I shouldn't have opened my mouth, but didn't I need to warn him? When I saw the look on Mr. Bantom's face and noticed how Mom bowed her head, I wanted to cry. Everyone within hearing distance watched him for a reaction. Dread shown on their faces.

"I shouldn't have done it," Michelle said softly, as she walked into the room holding Josie. "When Vinca told me that was wash water, I thought she meant for the clothes and diapers."

"No harm done, I guess," was Mr. Bantom's reply. The way he turned away from all of us made me believe he was hiding his true feelings about the situation.

"Let me get you a pan of fresh water," Mom said, before walking outdoors to the rain barrel. She came in and immediately put the pan on the rack over the fire so it could warm. "It'll only take a minute."

"No need. I can handle cold water. It's just the . . . well, you know, that I have a hard time with." Mr. Bantom lifted the pan from the fire and took it to the porch. I was sorry he'd experienced the baby poop, but I couldn't help feeling relieved it wasn't Paw who splashed the dirty water on his face. I ran to the porch with a towel for him to dry with. Mr. Mike and Mr. Derryhill were on the porch by this time, said their "good mornings" and went inside to get their breakfast. I remained on the cold porch.

"Mr. Bantom? Why is Paw being so mean to us? Why's he so upset?" I asked.

I could see movement in the distance, behind Mr. Bantom's cabin. It appeared that Paw was working on the repairs because he came around the corner of the cabin carrying trash for the burning pile.

"Oh . . . your Paw will get over it. He and I just have a difference of opinion. That's all. He's not mad at you. He's mad at me."

Mr. Bantom dried his face and led me back inside the warm cabin. I wasn't sure what their disagreement was about. Maybe it referred to the conversation I overheard? But I hoped it would end soon.

About three in the afternoon, Paw came back home. He walked into the cabin and sat silently in front of the fire, rubbing his raw, red hands near the heat. Tippy settled on the floor beside him.

"Paw? Why can't we just go home?" Once again, I thought better of opening my mouth after the words came out. All eyes were on him. I think everyone wanted to know the same.

"Things ain't safe back home. We have to wait until the trouble passes."

"How long will that be?" I bravely asked.

"Don't know, Lulu. The radio's broken, so there's no way of knowing unless I sneak back home and take a look around." With that answer, he turned and faced the rest of the folks in the room.

"Please go ahead and do it!" Mrs. Derryhill shrieked. "We're all miserable! We're freezing, we're going to starve to death, that dog needs a bath, and that baby is driving us all crazy with its screaming!"

Michelle rose and took baby Josie into the bedroom, slamming the door behind her. Mom followed after her, with Mike close behind.

Mr. Derryhill firmly grabbed his wife's arm and whispered something in her ear. Her face flushed slightly. She tripped on some bags on the floor as she walked away from him.

"Come on guys," I said to Roy Boy and Timmy. "Let's go outside and play." They must've thought it was a good idea because there was no hesitation in following me out the door. The cold air and open spaces were a welcome relief to the cramped, stuffy cabin. The three of us played hide and seek and talked about all the things we missed back home. Tippy spoiled the game for me by following me everywhere I hid.

We found our ball on the ground where it had rolled under the porch and proceeded kicking it back and forth between us. I noticed the cabin door opening. Mr. Bantom walked out with Paw close behind him. I crossed my fingers and hoped that the two of them got their disagreement settled so life would be calmer. I slipped away from the game, unnoticed, as Roy Boy and Timmy continued kicking the rubber ball as far as they could, chasing after it across the clearing.

Mr. Bantom and Paw settled on the porch of Mr. Bantom's burnt cabin, deep in conversation. I'm not proud of myself, but I snooped on them by hiding behind the charred wall of the cabin so I could hear what they were saying. I checked for spiders and then sat on an upside-down paint can.

"Roy, it's time for you to let these people go back home. This is getting ridiculous. You cain't trick them folks forever, just because of your mistake."

Paw was quiet for a moment before speaking. "If you hadn't blackmailed me, there'd be no problem going back."

"I didn't blackmail you, and you know it. It was a fair business deal, and you agreed to the terms. I won't let your family starve. But they surely will if you keep up this charade. And another thing. Don't go thinking you'll sneak back into town for anything. That garage is mine, and I don't want you going back there. For all I know, you'll burn the place down outta spite. Let us go home, or I'll tell them the truth."

"And just what is the truth, Bantom? What is the truth? That you blackmailed me out of my garage, and you're a snake? You believed in the cause just as much as I did."

"The truth is, mister, that you're keeping everyone prisoner because you can't go back and face your failure. That's the truth. I'll lead the whole lot of them back if that's what it takes."

"You know what I'll do if you try that." Paw's voice sounded sinister.

"So, you mean to tell me you'd shoot all of us, including your own family, just to keep from facing the music? Huh? And you'd better be careful about shooting anything at all. I didn't want to break this to you, but remember all that popping when my cabin was burning? That was our ammo. I had it stored along the back wall, and a little in that lean-to. It's ruined. We're gonna starve to death if we stay here."

Paw didn't say anything else. I scratched my arms raw and wanted to run to Mom, but I couldn't let him know what I'd heard. I didn't entirely understand what they were talking about but knew enough to feel scared to death. I waited until the two of them left, then I ran to my cabin as fast as I could.

— • ● • —

I stayed in the cabin for the rest of the afternoon, trying to occupy myself with anything that would take my mind off of Paw's words earlier. I watched as Mom worked making a broth for dinner. She pulled some bones out of the boiling water and tossed them into the sink. My eyes followed the snaking steam rising from the pot and wished we were in my kitchen back home. I missed the days of helping Mom with dinner preparation. Mom was a whiz at making simple ingredients into a feast. I was always amazed at how she knew what ingredients to use and how long to bake a casserole without a recipe in sight. Boy, how I missed the smell of Mom's turkey stuffing on Thanksgiving! And her apple pie! The one tasty thing I could still count on here was fresh-baked bread. We had half of a bucket of wheatberries remaining, so once or twice per week, Mom baked a loaf using a cast iron Dutch oven over the fire. On those nights, we each got one piece only. Mom was always careful about cutting the pieces in equal sizes to avoid any complaints. She kept one heel of the bread loaf for Timmy and one for Roy Boy. These were their favorite parts. The thought made me hungry. However, it appeared we would have only carrot slices and chopped, boiled eggs to go with our broth. Lately, there had been some talk of eating our last two remaining hens, but Mom convinced everyone they'd be more valuable for the eggs they provided.

I stayed close to Mom the rest of the evening. The discussion I heard between Paw and Mr. Bantom earlier disturbed me to the point of tears.

"What's the matter, Honey?" Mom asked as we put away the last of the dinner dishes.

"I'm just sad and missing home," I told her, not wanting her to know anything about the secret Paw was hiding and the threat Mr. Bantom accused him of. Although

I didn't fully understand what had transpired between the two men, I knew it was terrible enough to scare Paw into being mean toward all of us.

My prayer before bed was extra-long that night. Mom came in while I was saying it and later asked why I went silent halfway through. I told her I had drifted off to sleep, and the answer seemed to satisfy her. The truth is, I was silently asking God to calm my fears.

The next morning, Paw stood in the middle of the cabin's living room rapping a wooden spoon on the table while everyone was eating breakfast. The banging of the spoon got louder and louder until we realized he was trying to get our attention. He stopped, we all put down our eating utensils as he cleared his throat and looked at Mr. Bantom.

"We need to have a meetin' this evening, right here, after we eat dinner. Got some things to discuss. Okay?"

"What about our devotions? We haven't had a devotion for a while, Paw," I said.

"Why don't you come up with a devotion for us to do before our meetin', Lulu. That can be your job," he replied.

I wasn't sure what to think about his idea. It frightened me. Roy Boy rolled his eyes and turned to Timmy; they both chuckled.

"What's she gonna talk about? Her make-believe friend? Or maybe about how she cheats when we play cards." Timmy laughed at Roy Boy's comments, then looked at his mother who nodded and held her finger up to her mouth to tell him to be quiet. She seemed to be suppressing a smile, however.

"I'm sure Lulu can think of something good," Paw said.

"I look forward to hearing your words of wisdom, Effie," Mr. Bantom loudly declared as he gave me a hearty wink. "You're a smart girl. Now if you all don't mind, I'm gonna go work around my cabin." As soon as he left, Paw walked outside carrying his rifle. I watched out the window, concerned for Mr. Bantom, but Paw sat in a chair on the porch and remained there, staring off in the direction of his cabin.

I immediately busied myself, constructing something to say during devotion time. Now was my chance to speak from my heart and impress my parents with my maturity. Mom once told me I was wise beyond my years, and I didn't want to let her down. With a pencil in hand, I thumbed through the Bible. There were so many long, strange words I didn't understand, so I rummaged through my book box until I came across a Bible storybook my aunt gave me when she visited us from Ohio one Christmas. I had not looked at it since we first arrived at camp, I and found that flipping through the pages and seeing the colorful drawings of Bible characters gave me a sense of peace. There was Adam and Eve.

Looming behind them was a snake with a sneaky look on his face. A few chapters over, David stood in front of the giant Goliath. Goliath bared huge, white teeth as he grinned at the tiny David, who stood sizing up a stone he held in his hand. Sometimes I identified with David. When I was lost in the woods, I understood my smallness against the vastness of the forest. I never would've made it without God staying with me, protecting me from my "giant". I flipped back to the front portion of the book and felt a touch of fear as I looked at the drawing of Moses, holding the stone tablets on top of the mountain.

Lightning bolts zig-zagged down to the tablets. Fingers reached from the fiery bolts, etching words into the stone. My mind went back to the movie about Moses and the bloody water flowing through Pharaoh's palace. I shivered. I remembered Mom reading me many of these stories before bed, but she must've skipped over some of the scarier ones. *Maybe I could talk about Noah and the ark!* That seemed fitting to me because they all lived together in the ark waiting for disaster to come. *We are here at camp because we want to be protected from disaster.*

I sprawled out on the cabin floor for most of the afternoon, putting words to paper for the evening's devotion. When I read back what I'd written, it didn't make any sense to me.

"What time is it, Mom?"

"It's about dinner time, 5:00," was her answer. "I need for you to start setting the table for me, Effie. You'll need to put that stuff away now."

I panicked. My devotion wasn't ready for the meeting after dinner. This could be my one chance to speak my mind, and I'd failed. I said a silent prayer to God, asking for His help. I got up and gathered the plates for dinner and set them on the table.

"Plates or bowls, Mom?"

"Both," she said. "We're having bread with our soup tonight."

That news made me happy for two reasons: the bread was yummy, and the extra dishes to wash and put away would buy me a little extra time to come up with wise words for tonight.

We gathered around the fire, the kids sat on the floor while the grown-ups pulled chairs over. Michelle walked back and forth across the room, bouncing baby Josie in her arms to keep her quiet. Mr. Bantom set a footstool in front of the circle and gave me a pat me on the back.

"There's your seat, Miss Effie. I look forward to hearing what you have to say." He smiled and winked at me. I was beginning to grow very fond of him after thinking he was so ruff and gruff for most of my life.

I sat and hoped no one noticed my hand shaking as I held my piece of paper.

"Um. Noah took lots of animals on his ark because God told him to. He always minded God, so God saved his family. People made fun of Noah because he was building a big boat. I guess that's kind of the same thing Paw was doing when he brought us up here. I suppose God told him he needed to save his family even though some people laughed at him. Did they, Paw?" Paw nodded. "But I think the animals obeyed and were happy that Noah saved them on his ark. I don't think they fought, but I don't know for sure. And I bet the ark didn't smell very good either, just like it stinks in here when baby Josie poops." The group laughed. That was the first time I'd seen them laugh in a long time, and it felt good.

"Jesus told us to love our neighbor as ourself. When we yell at each other, we're not minding Jesus. I don't think

He's very happy when we act that way. I know I don't always obey, but I'm just a kid. It's not teaching us kids good things when we see grown-ups argue. From what I see, the adults need to learn from us kids how to get along. That's about all I have."

Mr. Bantom stood and clapped his hands vigorously. "Well done, Effie! I couldn't have said it better myself! You're a natural born teacher, little lady."

I was proud and embarrassed at the same time. Being the center of attention wasn't comfortable, but I liked the feeling of courage that washed over me. Now I had a little understanding of how the disciples in the Bible were strengthened by the Holy Spirit and able to speak to groups of people about Jesus.

Paw stood and shuffled from foot to foot, not making eye contact with anyone.

"Thanks, Lulu. Good job. Now we need to talk about some other things. As Lulu said, we all need to be considerate to each other and quit fighting because we'll be up here at camp for a while longer."

I noticed the rage in Mr. Bantom's eyes as he stared at Paw.

"It's my job to make sure everyone is safe, so I don't want anyone talking about going back to Burnt Willow until trouble passes. I know it ain't too fun, and it's getting pretty cold, but I need your cooperation. I don't want anyone thinking about leaving or sneaking back to town. There ain't nothing but trouble back there, and if anyone leaves . . . well, you'll be sorry."

Mrs. Derryhill gasped, and Mom bowed her head. I wasn't sure if Paw meant they'd be sorry about what they found back in Burnt Willow, or that he'd make them sorry for trying to leave. Either way, I didn't like what I heard, and it was obvious no one else did, either.

Mr. Bantom rose to speak, and Paw shot him a look that would kill.

"What Roy here doesn't want you to know is that the only trouble back home is the trouble that's waiting for him. Not you."

"Sit Bantom!"

Paw's demand was so loud and fierce, Michelle began to weep. Baby Josie joined right in screaming her head off. No one else made a noise. Paw stood and looked at each of us as if he were daring anyone to defy him. Mom was the first to rise. She fixed her eyes on him, turned and left the cabin, slamming the door behind her.

"No need for anyone else to leave the cabin. I'll go. But I won't be far. I'm going to keep my eye on you, so don't do anything stupid."

Paw turned and walked out, leaving us completely astonished by what we'd witnessed. We heard some loud, indistinguishable talking in the distance outside, then Mom returned to the circle of people. Still no words were spoken as we watched her search for what to say.

"I can't tell you how sorry I am for his behavior. I don't know what this is all about, but I plan to get to the bottom of it very soon. Please feel free to stay here tonight if you like. You're all welcome. We'll keep the fire going so you can stay warm. It's turning very cold outside, and I don't want anyone getting sick."

She left and walked into the bedroom, closing the door behind her. I didn't feel like staying in the living room without her, so I inched my way toward the bedroom. Roy Boy jumped up from his seat on the floor and followed me. I tapped on the door, then gently pushed it open and saw Mom sitting on the bed with her head in her hands, her feet dangling off the end. My brother and I sat on either side of Mom and put our arms around her. She patted our legs, and I could see that her eyes were red from crying. I realized at that moment that seeing your mother crying was the second most insecure thing in the world to me. Being without her in the woods was the only thing worse.

"It'll be alright," she whispered to us. I wasn't sure if it was the right time to speak or not but chose to anyway.

"Mom? What did Paw mean that we'd be sorry? And what trouble is waiting for Paw back home?"

She was quiet for such a long time without answering, and I was beginning to feel ashamed for asking. Mom sighed, took a couple of deep breaths, and looked back and forth at each of us.

"I don't know what's going on with your Paw, but I know that nothing will happen to either of you as long as I'm here. I'm convinced that your Paw loves you very much and is under a lot of stress. When the time is right, I'll talk to him and try to get to the bottom of it."

She spoke to us in such a grown-up way that it wasn't particularly comforting to me. I wanted to hear the usual; that Paw was just having a bad day and would be his old self after a good night's sleep. Or maybe that once we got back home, life would be normal again. But I was beginning to wonder if I'd ever see our house in Burnt Willow again.

Tippy walked in and stared at Mom anxiously.

"Kids, please go let Tippy out to do his business. And

don't roam away from the cabin."

I was eager to get outside and away from the somber atmosphere. As we passed through the rest of the cabin, Mrs. Derryhill remained uncharacteristically quiet. Timmy gave us a pleading look — I think he wanted to join us — but his mother pulled on his shirt every time he tried to take a step in our direction. Mr. Derryhill and Mr. Bantom were in a deep conversation, and all I caught of it was Mr. Bantom saying, "Ain't my place to tell you. You need to talk to him". Once we got on the porch, I perused the property as far as I could see in the flashlight's beam but didn't see Paw. The entire time Roy Boy and I were outside, however, I had the feeling we were being watched. Tippy became frisky and ran around the chicken pen a few times, sniffed the ground, and began following a scent trail away from the cabin's immediate area. I called to him a few times, but he ignored me until I heard Paw's voice yell out.

"Mind her and get back inside! And get that stinkin' dog. That da-- creature has scared off nearly every bit of wildlife in this camp ever since we came here! If we starve to death, it'll be that dog's fault!"

I wasn't sure from which direction his voice came, but Tippy took him seriously and ran back to the porch. Once inside, I noticed that Michelle was putting the baby in the make-shift crib we made from a cardboard packing box. Mom was puttering around the cabin. Along with her, she took the gazes of everyone sitting in the room. I tried distracting everyone by suggesting we play charades, but most claimed to be tired and ready for some shut-eye.

Surprisingly, Paw entered the cabin door a short time later. Sat down on one of the wooden chairs surrounding the dining table, then rose and packed a tea ball full of some leaves from the canisters and poured hot water in a mug. I tried to tell, by the aroma, what flavor he had chosen, but the only fragrance I could detect wasn't anything I recognized as the usual teas we drank. After dunking the ball for a while, he sipped a little from his spoon before grabbing for the sugar to sweeten it. He seemed satisfied, and I hoped the hot tea would calm his nerves.

"What's everyone staring at? Ain't you seen anyone drink tea before?" Immediately, everyone turned their eyes away from him and shuffled in their places a little, before resuming talk of being sleepy and wanting to get ready for bed.

Mr. Derryhill rose and grabbed his things. He nodded to his wife and Timmy who both obediently stood and seemed eager to leave and not stay the night.

"See you in the morning," Mom said as they headed out the door with their bags. "But you know you can stay here by the fireplace if you get too cold."

They nodded and left. Timmy ran back in and hugged me and Roy Boy. *What brought that on?*

"I liked your talk tonight at the meeting," he said to me before scurrying to meet up with his parents.

Mr. Bantom, walked to Paw and said, "I need to talk to you a minute when you finish your tea." I thought he was very brave to approach him. Paw rose with his mug in hand, nodded his head sideways toward Mr. Bantom, and motioned for him to follow him to the porch. I watched from the crack of the doorway, feeling I needed to make sure no one got hurt. [I couldn't hear the words that were said between the two of them that evening, but when I was older, I was told of the following conversation which transpired on the porch].

"Just want you to know that I ain't said nothing to anyone about what's going on. That's for you to tell your family. But I suggest that you do it soon. I'm gonna give you three weeks before I'll round everyone up and take them back down the mountain to town."

Paw looked at Bantom to see how sincere he was, but said nothing in return.

"Them kids of yours and that baby don't need to be out here in the cold, starving to death because of your pride. Just think about it and do what's best for them. And you can quit making your threats. You're scaring everyone. I know you won't harm those people sitting in there. They're all friends and family. You're talking crazy out of your head, so stop it. If I see you lift one finger to do anything stupid, well, I'll protect them. Just sayin'. Remember, three weeks to do the right thing or I'll do it for you."

Mr. Bantom walked back into the warm cabin, almost hitting me with the door as he pushed it open. Paw remained on the porch a few minutes before coming in, too.

CHAPTER NINETEEN

The cabin grew colder and colder as the weather outside indicated winter was here to stay. No longer did we have any afternoons that were warm enough to play outside for very long, and darkness came over the camp earlier and earlier. Mom told me that Christmas was only a few days away. The funny thing was, I didn't care too much. She tried to explain that the true meaning of Christmas remained the same, no matter where we were living and no matter the circumstances. I knew this to be true, but my heart just wasn't in the Christmas spirit.

That evening, Mom suggested we all gather around the fireplace and sing carols. Paw joined us, and I think he even enjoyed it a little bit. We kids got together and began planning a Christmas program. It was Timmy's idea, and I admit it gave me something to look forward to and got me in the holiday mood more.

Paw had calmed down somewhat and was mellower around us the last few days. With it being too cold and icy outside to work on the finishing touches to Mr. Bantom's cabin repair, he'd stay inside with us more, sipping his tea in front of the fire to warm himself.

Timmy, Roy Boy, and I spent the evenings practicing the program we planned to perform on Christmas day. We tried to keep our rehearsals at a low level, so Paw wouldn't get irritated with us as we repeated lines over and over. I noticed Paw getting up frequently to head to the outhouse. He complained that his stomach cramped and said that because of our lack of a well-rounded diet, his system was protesting. Eggs and beans were the only protein source we had available to us, and our supply of canned vegetables was nearly depleted. Mom did the best she could and tried to put a positive spin on things by saying she needed to lose weight. Indeed, she was slimming rapidly, and it was difficult for me to remember how heavy her frame was when we first arrived at camp.

No mention was made of Santa Claus, and I was afraid to ask if we would have a visit from him this year. My intuition told me "no", and I overheard Mom say to Paw that she had hoped I would believe for a couple more years before the Christmas "magic" went away for me. What she didn't know was that Roy Boy had been teasing me, telling me that Santa wasn't real for the past few months. At first, I didn't believe him but now wondered if that was what Mom meant by the "Christmas magic". Actually, I was a little relieved to think there may not be any Santa, and he wouldn't be showing up at my home in Burnt Willow with a sack full of toys, only to find that I was no longer there.

As of two nights ago, our daily routine changed slightly. Paw told us that those who were not staying in the cabin were to come by every two hours and check in with him. He explained that it was to make sure everyone was well and not suffering from the cold weather and lack of food, but the talk behind his back was that he was really making sure no one had escaped. He warned that if someone failed to show themselves on time, he would go looking for them. When Mike and Michelle missed their "house call', as he named it, he wasted no time getting upset. Mom's eyes were as big and round as an owl's when Paw grabbed his gun and headed out the door. She didn't have time to explain to him that she had offered to keep baby Josie for a while so Michelle could make up a little lost sleep. He stormed up to their cabin and banged on their door so loudly we could hear it all the way back at our place. Mom was holding Josie, who was fast asleep, so she sent me to catch Paw and explain what was going on. I didn't make it to their cabin before Mike opened the door and was met by Paw and his rifle.

"What—" Mike took one look at Paw's stern face and said no more.

"Where's Michelle?" Paw demanded.

"She's sleeping . . . or was sleeping. I'm sure your banging woke her. The baby had her up all night."

"Do you know what time it is! You missed your 2:00 check-in. Why didn't you come down and tell us where she was?" Paw was relentless in his interrogation.

"I thought Vinca would let you know," Mike answered.

"Yeah, Paw, Mom sent me up here to catch you and tell you," I said.

"Why didn't you come and check in by yourself, Mike? You didn't stay up all night taking care of no baby like she did."

"I wanted to make sure nothing disturbed her. And it's so cold up here, I thought I could keep her warm," Mike said.

"We don't need you keeping her warm if you know what I mean. We don't need us anymore babies in the camp," Paw barked.

Mike looked at me, and then back at Paw. "That isn't what I meant by keeping her warm, Roy. Trust me, I don't want another one right now either. This isn't the environment I want to raise kids in."

Paw walked away without turning toward Mike and said, "Don't be late for the 4:00 check-in or you'll be sorry."

I ran along behind Paw as he stomped back in the direction of our cabin. He paused, and turned to the right, went into the outhouse and shut the door. I took this opportunity to run back and tell Mom that everybody was okay, so she wouldn't worry.

"How could you!" Mom yelled at Paw as he walked through the door. "How could you think they would run off and leave this precious baby? Have you lost your senses? What has happened to you? You're turning into a tyrant!"

Paw didn't acknowledge her comments and went to the herb canisters on the kitchen counter. He used his fingers to scoop out some leaves from the canister on the very end of the counter and poked it into the tea ball. Mom watched and said nothing as he went to the fireplace, lifted the kettle off the hook and filled his mug. When Paw wasn't looking, I inched my way into the kitchen to see what kind of tea he was fixing for himself, hoping he wasn't using up the spearmint. Mom had marked the canister "chamomile".

I lifted the lids and began sniffing each, finding it soothing to draw in the familiar smells. When I got to the third one in line, I sniffed, then I sniffed again, because this one smelled like chamomile to me. I went to the end canister, the one Paw used, and lifted the lid. Although I detected some chamomile aroma, it also smelled like one or two other herbs as well. Had it been so long since I last played the guessing game with Mom, that I could no longer tell the difference?

"Mom? Have you changed some of the herbs around? This one don't smell like feverfew, and this other one don't smell like calendula. But this one is definitely spearmint," I said, tapping the next-to-the-last one. "My favorite. Can I make some tea?"

"Effie, I'll make it for you when Paw's finished with the tea ball. I don't want you to ever do this by yourself. You might burn yourself with the hot water."

I was confused because Mom taught me how to make tea by myself and allowed me to do it several times in the past. Maybe she was saying this for Timmy's sake since he was sitting nearby listening to our conversation.

Paw walked out onto the porch and tapped the wet, spent leaves from the ball onto the ground. He handed the ball to Mom without saying a word. Paw walked to the canister of sugar and filled his spoon twice before stirring vigorously. Mom walked to the wash basin and rinsed the ball well, then washed it again. She used a spoon to carefully fill the ball with leaves from the spearmint canister.

"I'm assuming you want your number one favorite?" she asked. I nodded.

The tea tasted so good, warming me as it went down my throat.

"That sounds good," Mrs. Derryhill said, watching me enjoy my cup. She walked into the kitchen space and asked Mom about the different teas she offered, before deciding on the same type I drank.

"I'll fix it for you," Mom said as she started the steeping process again for Mrs. Derryhill. "Now don't you go messing around with the herbs yourself or you might end up making a tea outta something unpleasant. Some of these herbs are strictly for medicinal purposes, so don't let Timmy go into these, either. Okay?"

"You'll have to tell me about their uses sometime, Vinca." I couldn't tell if she was truly interested or just pretending. She hung over the mug as steam rose. "My, that's an inviting smell. Reminds me of candy."

Mrs. Derryhill carried her mug over to the chair she had been sitting in and carefully lowered herself to sit. After wrapping a blanket around her shoulders, she cupped her hands around the hot mug and shivered a bit. Funny, but I hadn't heard her complain about the cold since Paw had turned mean.

At 3:45, Mike and Michelle came through the cabin door. Without a word, Mike sat while Michelle went into the bedroom to check on Josie, who was just beginning to cry after taking a nice, long nap. Michelle closed the bedroom door behind her, and I'm assuming she was feeding the baby because the crying stopped immediately.

Paw came into the cabin next, took his hat off, pulled off his boots, and set them by the fireplace. Mr. Bantom looked exhausted as he entered and walked to the wash basin to clean his hands.

"Let me warm some water for you," Mom said as he dunked his hands in the cold water.

"This water feels warm compared to the air outside, but thanks anyway," he replied.

"How's the cabin coming along?" she asked.

"'Bout got it ready for habitation. It'll be cold, but I'll have a roof over my head and four walls to keep the wind and rain out. Can't ask for anything more, except a fireplace would be nice!"

"You're always welcome to come here any time and warm yourself," Mom said. "That goes for all of you."

Paw grunted and said, "Where's Michelle?" There was gruffness in his voice as he glanced around the cabin living space.

"She's in the bedroom with the baby!" Mom shouted at him. I believe this was this first time I'd ever heard Mom raise her voice in anger.

"Okay. You can all go now. See you at 6:00 for dinner check-in," Paw told the group. No one budged. He sighed and went back out the door to continue at whatever he was doing earlier. I assumed he had been helping Mr. Bantom with the cabin, however, Mr. Bantom remained with us.

Mom began preparing dinner, while Mr. and Mrs. Derryhill napped in front of the fire. Timmy, Roy Boy, and I played a board game with Mike, and were later joined by Michelle who held Josie. In no time flat, Michelle rose with baby Josie and carried her into the bedroom, leaving a familiar trail of aroma behind. Mom heated some water, mixed some soap into it, and slowly carried the basin to the bedroom. I held my nose and opened the door for her. Mom carefully set the basin down on the floor next to Michelle, who held the dirty diaper in her hand. I quickly closed the door and went back to the game in the living room.

"I played your turn for you," Roy Boy told me as I sat.

"You coulda waited just a minute!" I shouted at him.

"Kidding . . ." he replied as I lifted my hand to hit him. "It's your turn, so go."

Mom came back into our room and washed her hands before continuing to chop vegetables. I was excited to hear her chop because that meant we would be having something with fresh ingredients instead of the broth with dried herbs and roots we foraged before the weather turned brutally cold, which had become the daily fare.

After the game was finished, Roy Boy, Timmy, and I went into the bedroom to have our dress rehearsal for the Christmas program, which we would be performing the next morning. Timmy complained loudly about the smell and said all his lines with fingers tightly clamped on his nose. At 6:00, we made sure we were in the other room waiting for Paw to check on us.

Dinner was ready and sitting on the table, but Paw still had not arrived at the cabin. I looked outside to see if I spotted him. He was nowhere in sight. I stood on the porch, not daring to leave and search for him when I saw the door of the outhouse open. I scampered back inside and took my place at the table.

Once Paw was in place, Timmy blessed the food, and the adults began passing the large pot of porridge around. Mom had already served the kids' bowls, which was her routine, to keep us from burning ourselves, she said. I figured she was really doing it to keep us from picking out all the good stuff in the soup. She carefully planned how many "chunks" we could each have.

I remembered how she tactfully took Timmy's bowl away from him the last time we were able to serve ourselves and picked out several pieces of carrot, placed them back in the pot, then handed his bowl back to him.

"I just want to make sure your folks have enough, too," she said to him that evening. I admired how she avoided any sneers from Mrs. Derryhill by turning it back as a kind gesture toward her. And this is why I think she changed her mind about allowing us to serve ourselves.

"Potatoes and carrots and turnips? Yum, Mom!" I said, stirring the soup in my bowl.

Paw cleared his throat before speaking. "Well. It's happened." He paused and looked at Mr. Bantom before continuing. "Martial law. The government finally did it. Heard it just now on the radio." He didn't look up from his soup, which he slurped with gusto.

Mr. Bantom took a deep breath and sighed.

I didn't believe a word Paw said and didn't understand why he said it. This time, it wasn't my intuition telling me it was a lie. I knew it for a fact. When I played with the radio yesterday, listening to my music station, I accidentally broke it. I knew Paw had not heard anything on the radio today or even late yesterday for that matter.

CHAPTER TWENTY

When I awoke on Christmas morning, it was still slightly dark outside but Mom had already gotten up. I heard soft footsteps in the living room, and saw her walk past the bedroom door, which she must've left ajar so she wouldn't wake me by shutting it. She pushed the door fully open and told me to get up because Santa Claus had paid a visit during the night. I couldn't believe my ears and amazed at how clever the bearded old man was to find us in the middle of nowhere. I grabbed Bear Bear from my cot and ran to see what she was talking about.

Mom told me that the adults had gotten up earlier, allowing the kids to sleep while they helped Santa get things ready for us. Timmy was still lying in his sleeping bag in the corner of the dining area, his eyes half-open. He saw my enthusiasm, wiped his eyes, and asked what was going on. I stood next to Roy Boy, his mouth hanging open as he stared at the fireplace mantle.

"Can you believe it! He found us!" I shouted at my brother as I yanked on his pajama sleeve.

Mom smiled and clapped her hands as we kids jumped around the room singing "Jingle Bells" at the top of our lungs. The fireplace looked like a scene from a Christmas storybook. It was the most beautiful, magical thing I'd ever seen with pine garland strung across and little candles lined up across the mantle. Red bows were tied to the garland in front of each candle. From four nails hung four red stockings. By the small bulge in each toe, I knew a present awaited each of us. "Roy Boy, this one's for you."

Roy Boy snatched it from Mom's hand, stuck his hand inside and pulled out a slingshot. He was speechless.

"Don't use it on any living thing," Mom cautioned, "or it will be taken away from you. Understand? Santa had to borrow my living-off-the-land reference books for all your gifts. He and the elves were used to making fancy baby dolls and roller skates."

"You mean he made it?" I asked Mom.

"It was a combined effort," she answered, looking at Mike.

"Is it my turn yet?" I asked, hopping up and down in front of her.

"Yes indeed," Mom said, pulling down another stocking. She looked inside, just to make sure, and handed it to me. "I had to teach the elves how to make this one."

I squeezed the toe and tried to guess what it could be. Then the thought occurred to me, *when did Mom meet with the elves?* I looked at Paw to see his reaction to Mom's comment about teaching the elves. He thought my friend Knock was make-believe at one time and threatened to harm him if he came near the camp. *Why did he allow elves to come near?*

I turned the stocking upside down and watched a small doll fall out onto the floor. I turned it around in my hands and noticed that its face was similar to Bear Bear's features except it had long eyelashes and a bow atop its head. I wasn't sure what type of animal the doll represented, but I loved it! I dashed to the kitchen and grabbed Mom's dishrag.

"Look! It matches! It looks like it was made outta the same stuff!"

"Santa thought Bear Bear needed a friend to play with, too," Mom said.

I picked Bear Bear up and started to introduce him to his new friend, but still wanted to know what type of creature it was so it could be named appropriately.

"What kind of animal do you think she is?" I asked Mom.

"Hm. Well, what kind of animal do you want her to be?"

"Maybe a dog like Tippy, except she doesn't have a tail. Probably just a bear like Bear Bear," I decided.

"I think that's a good decision. With her rounded ears, I think that's just what she is," Mom said.

"Bear Bear, meet Becky," I said, wagging the dolls at each other. "Nice to meet you," I said in an animated voice. "Welcome to Camp Marrying Tree. You'll like it here but stay away from Tippy. He'll try to play with you and get you all slobbery."

My comments seemed to amuse everyone. I had not realized I had become the center of attention, and it made me uncomfortable.

"Your turn, Timmy," I said. Mom lifted the next

stocking from the fireplace mantel and handed it to his eager hands. He reached in and pulled out a green object. The small tent he held looked like a miniature version of Mr. Chris' cabin when it had a tarped roof. In fact, I was sure it was the same fabric I saw covering the burnt part of Mr. Bantom's cabin after the fire. Timmy reached down further into the toe of his stocking and pulled out a little wooden man.

"Neat!" he said, placing the little man next to the tent he'd now set on the floor. "He can be a soldier, and this can be where he lives when he's not fighting."

"Or he can be a boy scout," Mrs. Derryhill said. "I think that might be a nicer thing to play, don't you?"

"No. He's a soldier," Timmy stated.

"I'm glad you all like your presents, but we need to get breakfast on the table now. So, stop the warfare boys and help me set the table," Mom said to Timmy and Roy Boy, who were shooting imaginary guns at each other.

"But Mom? There's one more stocking," I reminded.

"So there is. This must be for baby Josie," Mom said as she handed the stocking to Michelle, who had a huge grin on her face.

"Oh, Santa! That's so nice!" She found a small blanket stuffed in the stocking. The fabric matched the blanket on Mom's bed.

"Look, Mom! Santa must've used the same stuff we have to make things out of!"

"So he did! It's a small world!" Mom said. The adults chuckled at her comment. "Now it's time for us to eat."

For breakfast, we had eggs and homemade bread, warm from the fire. Mom told us she'd saved up enough eggs for us each to have two as a special Christmas blessing. I watched as she went to the pantry and pulled out a jar of blueberry jam she had hidden in the back. She turned to Mrs. Derryhill and handed it to her.

"Merry Christmas, Jane. I know how much you like this! Enjoy!"

I couldn't believe my eyes. Where did she find another jar of my favorite jam and why did she give it away? Mom was too generous for her own good. Mrs. Derryhill took the jar and popped the lid open.

"I think I'll enjoy some of this with that delicious bread! Would anyone else like some?" she asked.

Before Mom could object, I raised my hand and stated in a very loud voice, "I do!"

Mrs. Derryhill took a small piece of warm bread from the plate and spread the thinnest smear of jam on it, handed it to me and smiled.

"Here you go, Sweetie," she said.

"Thanks a lot," I said with an edge to my voice. I hoped that Mom would not pick up on my disappointment in Mrs. Derryhill's lack of generosity.

I licked the jam ever so lightly to make the enjoyment last.

"Stop eating like a dog, Effie. That's gross," Roy Boy said to me.

"Remember the Christmas spirit," Mom reminded. "Let's all try to be nice to each other today out of respect for baby Jesus' birthday."

I wondered if she was aiming those remarks at Paw, but he didn't seem to notice even though everyone turned their gazes toward him.

"When can we see your program?" Mr. Bantom asked.

"Oh, yes! Timmy has been practicing non-stop," Mrs. Derryhill said. Her husband nodded in agreement.

"After breakfast," Roy Boy answered. "But you'll have to give us time to get ready and in our costumes."

Paw lifted his eyebrows at that comment and cracked a smile. "Costumes . . . or blankets and towels?" He took a sip of his coffee and wiped a piece of his bread across the running yolk of his over-easy egg.

When the last breakfast dish was cleaned, the boys and I slid the dining table over to one side and asked everyone to sit in a row facing the fireplace. We huddled over last-minute directions from our director, Roy Boy, and went into the bedroom to slip into our costumes. Paw was right. Our costumes consisted of the blankets off the beds and anything else made of fabric which could be wrapped around us.

I leaned out of the bedroom door and yelled, "Tippy! Come!" Tippy lifted his sleepy head and looked at me with heavy eyes. "Tippy! Here! Here, boy!" I patted my legs until he plodded his way to me. I grabbed him and dragged him into the bedroom and shut the door.

"Okay. We have our camel," I said to the boys. "Throw that towel over his back and pin it, Roy Boy. I'll get the shepherd ready.

"I thought I was gonna be a king," Timmy whined.

"The kings don't do anything. The shepherds go find baby Jesus. Besides, we don't have any king clothes. A king can't be wrapped in a blanket. I'll be Mary and Roy Boy will be Joseph, just like we practiced. Now hurry up and let's get going." I handed Timmy the blanket off the cot, then pulled the sheet from the bed.

I wrapped the bedsheet around my body and over my head and handed Roy Boy a striped blanket — the one that matched baby Josie's new blanket. Since Santa, or Mom, cut a piece from it to sew the baby blanket, it almost didn't cover him completely.

"Ta da!" I shouted as Roy Boy and I emerged from the bedroom. We walked slowly around the room and ended up in front of the fireplace.

"I'm so tired Joseph, and I think the baby Jesus is getting ready to be born. We'd better find a place to stay. What about over there?" I said, pointing to a chair next to a bench I'd flipped over.

"Sounds good. The innkeeper said we can stay in the stable because they were full inside." I placed a thick towel across the legs of the upturned bench. Roy Boy helped me to the chair, then walked over to Michelle, who was rocking baby Josie in her lap. "We need to borrow her now," Roy Boy said to her.

Michelle handed Josie to Roy Boy, who looked terrified as he held her with stiff arms. Mom jumped out of her seat and tried to stop him.

"It's okay, Vinca. They told me what they were going to do, so we rehearsed holding her." She smiled and nodded at Mom, who sat back down.

Roy Boy handed the baby to me, and I started to place Josie on the towel that was stretched out between the legs. Mom rose again.

"Michelle! Don't let her—"

Michelle jumped up and grabbed Josie from me. I wasn't sure why because she said Josie could be baby Jesus.

"Honey, why don't you just let me hold her and use the new baby doll instead." Michelle handed the doll to me, and I placed it in the towel instead of Josie. The towel slipped off the legs of the bench, so I then understood why it wasn't a good idea.

"Oops. Sorry baby Jesus," I said to the doll as it landed on the bottom of the bench. "Pretend like that didn't happen," I addressed the audience. Everyone laughed. "And pretend like there's a star right there. I pointed to the mantle above where I sat. "You forgot to make a star!" I whispered to Roy Boy.

"Sorry."

"Well, the angels said that Jesus was born, and He was going to save the world by being born. Wise men came and brought the baby Jesus gifts of gold, Frankenstein . . . I mean frankincense, and myrrh." Everyone was laughing so hard they didn't hear my correction. I couldn't stop the tears from coming, so I turned my head and dabbed my eyes. "I changed what I said, but no one heard me say it right." I whimpered beneath my sobs.

Mom put her arms around me and held me tight. "You're doing a great job," she said, kissing me on the top of my head. "Everyone laughed because it was so cute. Now finish your play because we all want to see it. We've been waiting all morning."

I turned back around and said, "Well, I think that's about all we were going to do anyway." I then noticed the stricken look on Mrs. Derryhill's face.

"Where's Timmy? Isn't he going to do anything?" she said.

"Oh, yeah. There were shepherds in the field, watching

their sheep." I paused and waited. "There were shepherds in the field, watching their sheep," I said louder. Still nothing happened. "Hey, Timmy!" I yelled.

The bedroom door opened, and Timmy emerged, dragging Tippy along with him.

"The angels said we'd find you here." Timmy sat on the ground next to the makeshift manger; Tippy flopped down beside him.

"The shepherds went back, glorifying God. The end," I said.

Mr. Bantom rose to his feet, "Bravo! Bravo!" Everyone else followed suit, clapping loudly.

While walking back to the bedroom to change out of our costumes, I heard Mrs. Derryhill ask, "Is that all Timmy gets to do?" Then I heard a loud shhhh back at her. Probably Mr. Derryhill because he was always quieting her when she spoke out rudely.

———— •●• ————

Midday, after a lunch of thickened broth with dumplings, the grown-ups decided to take a nap close to the fire, and my thoughts turned to Knock. He was all alone somewhere in the woods. No one was celebrating Christmas with him. No presents waited for him under a tree. He had no stocking hanging from a fireplace. And worst of all, I suspected he had no family members to be with him on this special day. That needed to change. He just couldn't be alone while we stayed warm by the fire, having fun.

I had one hour before the mandatory check-in time with Paw. This would be enough time to find Knock and wish him a Merry Christmas. I grabbed a few nuts Mom toasted earlier and quietly left the cabin, heading in the direction of the marrying tree. I'd seen him there once before, so I gathered his home must not be too far away from that location.

The path down the hill took on a different look and sound now that winter had arrived. Branches on the bare trees rattled and creaked in the cold breeze and crispy brown leaves lined the once-cleared dirt trail. I found a stump near the marrying tree and sat, holding myself tight, tucking my cold hands under my armpits to thaw them. My mind wandered back to the cabin where I had left my warm gloves on the hearth in my haste to go look for Knock. I called Knock's name a few times and listened for a reply. The only sound I heard was the wind as it picked up speed and tossed the treetops back and forth. An occasional bird flew from branch to branch, but even the squirrels must've had enough sense not to be out on such a cold day as this. A rush of anxiety washed over me as I remembered the night I spent alone in the woods. Never again would I step one foot from a familiar path in the woods.

I called to Knock once again, then screamed "Merry Christmas, Knock!" at the top of my voice. "I left you some nuts Mom toasted this morning. They'll be sitting right here on this stump!"

I waved in all directions in case he was watching from afar. I figured he may not want me to know his location in case Paw went hunting for him. My lungs burned from the cold as I ran back up the hill toward camp. When I entered the clearing, I bent and caught my breath. No one must suspect that I'd wandered away from the cabin's vicinity, so I drew in a few long, deep breathes and gently pushed the cabin's door open, hoping not to wake anyone from their nap. I was horrified to see that no one was sleeping, and all heads turned in my direction as I entered.

"Do you know what time it is?" Paw said, not a bit of warmth was in his expression. "Where have you been? No! Don't tell me because I don't want to hear no lies! I know where you've been because I followed you! That'll be the last time you leave this cabin!"

"Roy!" Mom shouted. "How dare you threaten my daughter like that! And on Christmas!"

Paw turned to face Mom, and I'd never seen such rage in his eyes before. I clung to Mom, sobbing.

Mr. Bantom approached Paw and stood in front of him, almost nose-to-nose, lifted his pointer finger in Paw's face and seemed to struggle finding the words to say. He turned and looked at the other two kids, then jabbed Paw in the stomach with that out-stretched finger.

"If them kids and women weren't in here, you'd hear words come out of my mouth that would have you shaking in your boots, you bully ," he growled. "You don't treat any youngin' like that, especially one of your own! You hear me? We're packing up and leaving this place first thing in the morning. Just try to stop us!"

Paw walked to where his rifle stood propped against the wall, lifted it and pointed it straight at Mr. Bantom.

"Ain't no one leaving this place. No one is ever leaving this cabin until I say so."

Paw swept the rifle's long barrel around the room, not pointing it at anyone in particular, but no one was spared being in the path of its aim. I covered my eyes and whimpered. My trembling must've touched a nerve with Paw. He grunted at me and poked my arm, startling me. I slowly lowered my arm from my eyes and peeked at Paw. His reddened eyes didn't resemble the gentle brown eyes I remembered from this summer — the eyes that winked and crinkled at the corners whenever he saw me.

"Go boil some water for me. I want some tea." Paw walked to the far corner of the room and sat on a small, wooden chair; his rifle rested against his right leg.

"Yes, Paw," I said, my tear-filled eyes didn't turn away from him for more than a second at a time. Roy Boy walked next to me as I went to fetch the kettle and fill it with water drawn from the rain barrel the evening before. Mom bent to whisper to the both of us.

"Don't be afraid. I won't let anything happen to you. Trust me."

I noticed that Mrs. Derryhill had a terrified Timmy sitting in her lap. Mr. Derryhill placed a protective arm around his wife and pulled her closer. Michelle, Mike and baby Josie remained in the bedroom, where the three of them had napped before my walk to the marrying tree. From time to time, Mike peeked through the crack in the door to see what was going on.

When the water boiled, I took a mug to the fire and reached out to get the kettle. Mr. Bantom stepped in and lifted it off the iron rack for me and poured the steaming water into the mug.

"Don't want you getting yourself burned, Honey," he

said, replacing the kettle to the iron fireplace rack.

Paw stood and walked to the kitchen area and pointed at a particular canister. "I want some of that, mixed with some of that one on the end."

I looked at Mom. She nodded. "Give Paw the canisters he wants and let him mix his tea the way he likes it. It'll be okay."

She knew my hesitation. The herbs he'd picked out weren't typically used to make tea, but I wasn't going to argue with Paw.

"This one's gotta pretty good taste. And I like the bouquet of this one," he said, pointing toward the last canister. "Isn't that the way fancy people say it?" He cracked a faint smile.

I nodded in agreement without saying a word.

"Your Mom's always saying that these herbs are good for what ails you. She ain't the only herbal doctor around here. I need some herb tea medicine about now. My belly's been hurting."

Before Paw put the lid back on the canister, I peeked inside and noticed it was about empty. I took a deep breath and tried to remember which herb it was. *Is it feverfew?* There was so little of it left, I suppose most of the fragrance had left.

Paw walked over to the sugar canister and stirred a heaping spoonful into his tea. Lifting the mug to his lips, he drew in the aroma and let out a sigh.

"Um. Delicate bouquet. Reminds me of springtime. Hand me that sugar, Lulu. It tastes like the sugar ain't so sweet anymore. I need to add more."

I looked at Mom. She didn't seem phased even though

she'd told me we had to be very easy on the sugar supply because it was dwindling to an end. I looked into the canister, and it was filled halfway to the top with the white granules. I wanted to dip a spit-wet finger into the beautiful white stuff and pop it into my watering mouth but didn't dare do it when anyone was looking.

After his tea suited his taste, Paw pulled his chair closer to the waning fire and pulled his shoes off. His toes wiggled inside his grubby socks.

"Guess someone needs to bring in a couple more logs to throw on the fire. My toes are damp and cold." No one jumped to grant his wish.

"But Paw, you said no one could leave the cabin," I said before realizing my comment might sound like an attempt at being sassy.

"So, I did. I'll let Mike fetch the wood. Hey! Mike!" Paw yelled. Mike came out of the bedroom and stood in front of Paw. "Why don't you go get a couple of logs outta the stack next to the cabin and bring them in here? Do you mind?"

Without a word, Mike did as Paw instructed. Everyone watched as Mike removed the fire screen and tossed the wood onto the glowing embers. Sparks flew in all directions. Mr. Mike stomped-out one glowing speck that landed on the floor in front of the hearth and replaced the screen before going back into the bedroom to be with his wife and baby. No words were exchanged between him and Paw.

"Cat got everybody's tongues? Sure got quiet in here," Paw commented.

"Everyone's afraid to speak to you for fear of their

lives," Mom said back at him. "You ought to be ashamed of yourself acting like a crazy man. What's wrong with you anyway?"

I grabbed Mom's arm tightly, as I feared retaliation from Paw over her remarks, but Paw remained silent. I suspect Mom was the only one who could get away with telling him how hateful he'd become.

"I'm going to bed now." Paw dragged Tippy outside and tied him to the front porch with enough rope to do his business a few feet into the dirt area at the side of the cabin. He went to his toolbox and removed the hammer and a very long nail from the box's tray. He slid the large wooden bolt across and latched the door shut. We had never before latched the door because this cabin was considered to be everyone's place to come whenever a need arose. Paw nailed the wooden bolt to the door frame and shook it to make sure it was secure.

"I'd better find it just like this in the morning with everyone accounted for." Paw ran Mike and his family out of the bedroom and closed the door enough to leave a small slit so he could see the front door from his side of the bed.

As soon as Paw began snoring, Mr. Bantom motioned for everyone to gather around him.

"Something's up with Roy. He ain't behaving like himself. I think it's in everyone's best interest to go along with him for right now until he comes to his right mind. I'd hate to see anyone getting hurt. We're gonna leave this place, but we might ought to wait until we gain his trust again. If we tried to leave right now, someone will get shot. Something just ain't right with that man, so let's humor him until he settles down. Is everyone on board?"

All nodded their agreement with the plan.

"Do we have enough provisions to last a little while longer, Vinca?" Mr. Bantom asked.

"Things are getting' pretty low. We might be living off our own fat if we wait very long. I have one hen still laying, and a partial bucket of wheat left, so we'll have bread. My sugar supply seems to have miraculously replenished itself," she laughed, looking inside the cannister. "Don't know how that happened, but I guess if Jesus could multiply a couple of fish and a loaf or two of bread, He can increase our supplies! He is good and He will take care of us."

"Amen, Vinca," Michelle added. "The Good Lord is right here with us and won't let anything happen to His precious children."

"Merry Christmas everyone. I think we all need to turn in for the night. It's been a long day," Mr. Bantom suggested.

"Merry Christmas," we all replied before finding our spot on the floor to settle. I assumed we women would now be sleeping near the fire with the men. Tippy whimpered on the front porch. I went to the window and blew him a kiss and told him I loved him. Mom sat up for a long time after the lamp was shut off. I suppose she was trying to decide whether or not to join Paw in the bedroom. She bowed her head for a few minutes, then curled up on the floor next to me and Roy Boy. Although she boldly stood up to Paw earlier in the evening, I figured she didn't want to take a chance at waking him.

CHAPTER TWENTY-ONE

We were all aware that the sun was up, and Paw had not emerged from the bedroom to check up on us and take a headcount. By the haggard looks on the faces of the others, I assumed their sleep must've been as restless as my own. Mom got up before the rest of us but could not begin breakfast preparation until Paw gave us permission to leave the cabin. The fire went out sometime in the middle of the night, but no one dared leave the cabin to gather more logs.

Mom pushed the bedroom door open and approached the bed where Paw lay. I stood with her as she ever so slightly jostled his sleeping body. Paw stirred and groaned. He jabbered something I could not understand and curled himself into a fetal position. The smell in the room was worse than when Josie soiled her diapers.

"What's wrong?" Mom asked him.

"I don't know," Paw squeaked back. He cringed and held his stomach. "Been cramping all night. I had to use that bucket over there a few times. Been vomiting all night."

I held my nose and left the room. Paw was in no condition to be yelling or hurting anyone right now, so I felt

I could safely leave Mom in the room with him.

"Paw's sick. Been sick all night," I announced to the others.

Mr. Bantom walked to the front door and removed the nail Paw had hammered in. I gasped and thought he must be the bravest man I'd ever known. Mr. Derryhill watched intently as Mr. Bantom slid the bolt and opened the door. He untied Tippy and let him back into the cabin to warm himself.

"Think that's a good idea? You might get us all killed," Mr. Derryhill cautioned.

"He ain't in any condition to do anything about it. Poor animal's been whimpering all night," was all Mr. Bantom said as he exited. He returned with an armful of kindling. He dumped that in front of the fireplace and went back out. The cold rush of air was like a refreshing mountain stream flowing through the cabin, cleansing the air of the putrid smell that had seeped from the bedroom. Mom walked through the room with the bucket and carried it to the open door. I watched as she walked to the edge of the woods and dumped its contents into the brush, stopping to rinse the remaining bits of Paw's bile and excrement with the cup of wash water she took with her. She carried the bucket back into the room. I heard her ask Paw if he needed anything. He grunted something, and she went to the canister of chamomile to begin filling the tea ball.

Within a very short time, Mr. Bantom had a roaring blaze going. When slapping tongues of fire died down enough to begin boiling the water in the kettle, Mom began the familiar process of placing it on the iron rack until steam poured from its spout.

"Breakfast will be a little late this morning," she told all of us. No one minded, and I heard Mrs. Derryhill compliment Mom on her kind heart toward Paw. Kinder than she would have been, she remarked. Michelle handed baby Josie to Mike and went to the kitchen to start grinding wheat for the morning's loaf of bread. As of the last couple of weeks, we no longer had enough wheat and eggs to make pancakes, so Mom made sure she provided us with a crusty loaf of bread and a hot pot of coffee or tea. Mr. Bantom noted that the coffee was getting weaker and weaker. I know he didn't mean any harm by his comments because he chuckled and winked when he said it. I remember how Mom bought bags and bags of coffee beans at the store every time she went before we left for camp. At that time, I didn't understand why we needed so much of it or why Mr. Bantom would bring cash to the house and tell Mom it was to be used for anything we would be needing later on. Mom didn't realize I saw this, so I never asked what it was all about. In my innocence, I thought he was being benevolent toward the family and that Paw's business wasn't doing well.

Recently, I overheard Mr. Derryhill say something to the effect that if he'd known we'd all be starving to death in this miserable place, he would have insisted that everyone kick in more money for supplies, so we'd have a decent meal every once in a while. No one seemed to appreciate how hard Mom worked foraging and making the foodstuffs stretch. Paw, however, had commented on that over and over in his nicer days. Mom volunteered to do all the cooking, and she always did it with a smile on her face. But as of late, that smile became replaced by a look of exhaustion and worry.

While Mom was in the bedroom tending to Paw, Timmy made a confession to me. He didn't realize he was confessing anything bad at the time, but thought he was letting me in on a secret scheme I'd want to participate in.

"When no one was around," he told me, "I'd eat the sugar in the canister. I have a secret stash of it in my box of toys. Well, I did have a stash of it. It's almost gone now. Your Mom noticed that the sugar was getting low, so each day, I would take a little of that other white stuff and mix it in so the can would be fuller. Then I poured some of my sugar on top so she wouldn't notice anything missing anymore. Pretty smart, huh?"

"What other white stuff?" I asked him.

"There's another can of white stuff under the sink. It smells kind of good. Most of it's on the bottom. I covered it up."

"Did the other stuff have a bonehead on it?" I was horrified by his secret.

"Yeah. It had a pirate thing on it. How did you know?" Timmy asked.

"That bonehead stuff is poison! Mom uses it to kill vermin! We've got to tell her what you did!"

Timmy begged me to not get him in trouble and swore he wouldn't do anything else ever again. I felt so sorry for him. He meant no harm. I wondered if Paw had been getting down to the part of the sugar canister where the bonehead stuff was. I had to keep Paw from using the sugar but couldn't let him know Timmy's secret. That would be the end of my friend Timmy.

Paw stayed in bed the rest of the day and didn't seem

to care about our comings and goings. Mom said he was too sick to be ornery toward us, so the three of us kids took advantage of our freedom and played outside until time for dinner. We had our usual broth with one or two carrots boiled in it to make a soup. Mom made us a special treat of biscuits to go along with the soup. She said she believed our time at camp was drawing to an end, so she felt more confident about using the wheat for that purpose. I shuddered to think that we might try to slip out one night without Paw knowing we were leaving, and I certainly didn't want to leave Paw at camp by himself, even though being around him frightened me.

After dinner, everyone, with the exclusion of Paw, gathered in the living room for an evening devotion. Paw remained in bed, so Mom got up every so often to check in on him. Mike and Michell led the devotion time for the first time and prayed for Paw. I hoped that he was listening. They spoke of how forgiving God is toward us when we aren't obedient and how we must turn from our ways and how we need to be forgiving of others just the way God is toward us. Mom's eyes glistened with tears while listening to them. I wondered if she was thinking about Paw. Surely the devotion didn't convict her heart as she has been nothing but kind toward Paw. But on the other hand, I suspect the rest of the group harbored ill feelings and would gladly leave him here to freeze or starve to death if it meant freedom from this awful life. I, myself, struggled with feeling compassion one hour and contempt the next. I loved my father immensely, but that love waned when I saw his treatment of the people who shared the camp with us.

Mom suggested that anyone who desired the heat of

the fireplace continue sleeping in the living area of our cabin, of course unless they preferred to go back to their own cabins and bundle up against the sub-freezing temperatures. Only Mr. Bantom left. Mike and Michelle offered use of their cabin since his still had an unfinished wall and was surely draftier than theirs. Mom assured everyone that Paw had nothing contagious and didn't seem to be running a fever that she could detect. The risk of freezing must've been greater than the risk of catching a deadly disease as everyone else chose to stay by the fire for the night.

I'm not sure where Mom slept, or even if she did sleep, because every time I woke up, I was aware of her pacing back and forth between the bedroom and her chair by the fireplace. At some point, I fell into a deep sleep and dreamt about Knock. In my dream I met him by the marrying tree and told him about Paw's illness and how Paw had turned mean toward his loved ones and friends. Knock spoke. *Had I ever heard his actual voice before?* I wasn't sure. But after thanking me for the nuts I left him on the tree stump, he asked me how my Christmas morning was. I told him about the play, the gift in the stocking, and how Paw started threatening all of us at the point of a gun. He frowned and put his hand on my shoulder. He didn't seem surprised by any of it but assured me that I needn't worry. Then he said something else. Something that troubled me very much. He told me that he would never be meeting me at the camp again but that I would understand some day. That his work was almost over. When I started crying, he told me not to be sad but to be glad that everything would be back to normal soon. I never thought to ask him about his work or where he'd been living. But, for some strange reason, I thanked him. I felt an overwhelming sense of gratitude toward him. Exactly for what reason, I didn't know. I gave him a tight hug and he told me to hurry and get back home. I woke from the dream confused because it was so vivid. *Was it a dream or did I really meet with Knock and have this conversation?*

After my morning piece of bread, I went into the room to see Paw. His gaunt face seemed pale and hollow. His beard was in bad need of grooming and his lips were cracked and thin. He turned to look at me and smiled.

"Don't worry none about your Paw. I probably look like death warmed over, but I'll be okay. Must've eaten something that didn't agree with me."

"Can I get you some water or tea, Paw? Mom always gives me chamomile when my tummy hurts."

"Thanks, Lulu, but Mom brought me a cup of water. It's sitting right here on the table. Has anyone else gotten sick from the food?"

"No," I answered.

"Maybe someone's trying to poison me," he said. "I wouldn't blame them."

I think he was joking but then again, he didn't smile when he said it. His words reminded me of the confession Timmy made and how Timmy put the boneface stuff in the sugar canister.

"What time is it?" he asked. I told him that I forgot to wind the clock that morning, but it must be about eleven o'clock or so. His expression darkened.

"Tell everyone to come into my room at three o'clock and check in with me. And tell them that I may be sick, but

I still don't want any deserters."

I assured him that everyone was at the cabin for coffee and bread and had no plans to run off and leave camp. I told him that everyone was concerned about him and asked how he was doing. That was only part of the truth, however, as I overheard Mrs. Derryhill say to her husband that it would be a blessing if he died. She said that we should all make a run for it now that he was no longer a threat to us. Never had I wanted to kick anyone more than I did at that moment.

I told Paw I'd check on him later in the day and would be sure to see him at three o'clock, so he'd know I didn't run off and leave camp. After leaving his room, I shut the door and looked around making sure no one saw me grab my coat and exit the cabin.

Apprehension filled me on the walk down the hill. *What if we leave camp and I never see Knock again?* In the dream, Knock told me his job was almost finished and that I wouldn't be seeing him again. Was that because we would be leaving him or, was he leaving us?

When I reached the stump near the marrying tree, I saw that the nuts I left there were missing. Knock had removed them, I was sure. Roy Boy told me that once, he saw me walk around the cabin while sound asleep, so it was possible that I had, indeed, met with Knock last night. But it wasn't nighttime in my dream. The sun was shining, and the birds flitted in the trees. But strangely, it was timeless. I felt as if I'd spent the entire day with him, but yet very little conversation was made beyond my jabbering on and on about Paw, and Knock's replies that were meant to put my mind at ease.

I waited at the stump and hoped I would see Knock,

but my intuition told me that those words he spoke in my dream were true. Knock had left, and I would never see him again. The woods no longer held any fascination for me. A lonely, empty feeling swept over me as I walked back uphill toward camp.

Mom was washing a mug in the kitchen when I entered the cabin.

"Close it quietly and gently," she cautioned. "We don't want to wake your father."

Three o'clock came, and people started gathering for check-in. Mr. Bantom never arrived at the cabin. Mike went to look for him and reported back to us that he found him packing up supplies in his cabin.

Paw slept through the three o'clock check-in. Mom said that after his mug of tea, he asked that no one bother him because he was sleepy. I motioned for Mom to follow me into the kitchen, as I had something important to tell her.

"Did you put sugar in Paw's tea?" I asked.

"Of course, I did. He won't drink it any other way."

I struggled to find the words to say. Timmy watched me as I huddled with Mom.

"Um. Maybe you shouldn't give Paw any more tea."

"That's a strange thing to say. What's the matter?" she asked.

"Someone might've done something bad."

"Effie, are you in trouble? What are you telling me?"

"Someone's been sneaking sugar to eat and was afraid of getting in trouble, so they put boneface stuff in the canister because it is white, too. I know Paw ain't vermin, but I don't think he should be eating any of the sugar anymore."

"Effie? Did you put poison in the sugar canister?"

"No ma'am. I didn't do it, but I can't tell you who did because I promised."

Mom was quiet. She looked inside the boneface canister, then opened the sugar canister and stirred the contents with a spoon.

"When did this person do this?" Mom whispered to me.

"I saw him messing with the canister a few days ago," I said.

"No harm done," was her response. I think we've eaten all the good sugar off the top, so no one has gotten to the poison yet."

I was relieved that no one was to blame for Paw's illness but couldn't help but wonder if Mom was just pretending not to be worried. Mom walked over to where the rest of the group sat and announced, "I don't want anyone touching the sugar canister. It's not safe for us to use the sugar. Something accidentally fell in it."

Michelle looked up from where she sat, holding a sleeping Josie. "Do you think Roy got into it and got sick?"

"He's been feeling poorly for a while now. Roy is sick because he's eaten something that didn't agree with him, so whoever put the poison in the sugar, I mean contaminated the sugar, isn't to blame. Roy is a grown man and is responsible for his own actions. If he did eat some of the poison, no one knew better and neither did he, but I think the consequences would've been worse if we'd told him what happened. I still think he ate something that made him sick. He did it to himself. Probably got hungry and shot a squirrel or something. Those things have got to be cooked well before eating them, or they'll make you sick. Do you all understand? He brought this illness on himself, so I don't want anyone feeling guilty."

"Poison?" I heard Mrs. Derryhill say. "My Timmy could've died if he'd gotten into it! Why aren't you more careful with our foodstuffs? You know kids will get into anything sweet!"

I looked at Mom to see if she would defend herself, but she remained quiet for a minute. When I opened my mouth, she must've known I was going to tell on either Timmy or Roy Boy and stopped me before the first syllable came out.

"We just all need to be more careful," she said softly.

"What are we going to do now? It's bad enough that we're all starving to death. Now we can't even enjoy a cup of coffee without sugar to use! That was the last thing we had to look forward to. I can't drink it without sugar," Mrs. Derryhill whined.

"Don't blame Mom!" I shouted back. "Timmy—" Mom shot me a "shut-up" look, so I knew not to continue.

Timmy's bottom lip quivered, and he fixed his big, reddened, glassy eyes on me. He mashed himself so tightly against his mother, pulled his legs up to his chest and wrapped his arms around them until he turned into a round, little bundle. I believe he would've rolled right off the couch if his mother didn't have such a tight hold on him.

Mom left the room to check on Paw. She came out of his room and started flipping through all her herb books, reading some of the pages very intently.

"Are you gonna make Paw some of your herbal medicine, Mom?"

She didn't answer me right away, so I asked her again,

then she closed the book.

"Have you seen which herbs your Paw has been making his special tea out of?" she asked. She opened a few of the cans and peered inside. "Just as I thought."

"Well . . . I think he got some of this one and this one," I said, tapping the side of the cans. "But he had some of this one, too. I told Paw those weren't tea herbs, but he said they tasted good, and he wanted something to make his tummy feel better. He said he knew what he was doing and told me to be quiet."

"And you did the right thing, Honey. No one can tell your Paw what to do," Mom said calmly.

"Is he gonna be okay?" I asked.

"God is in charge and won't allow anything to happen that isn't His will. He's in God's hands, so he'll be okay. Don't worry, Honey."

I looked around at everyone in the room. Mrs. Derryhill didn't seem concerned about anyone but herself and her little frightened Timmy. Roy Boy played himself in a game of checkers in the corner of the cabin. Mr. Bantom and Mr. Derryhill were both asleep in their chairs, taking their usual naps. Mike was carrying in firewood and setting it next to the hearth. I seemed to be the only one worried, which offered me a little comfort because maybe I needn't be so afraid. I wished that I could clear out of my mind the image of weak, pale Paw, lying on the bed. Other than an occasional trip to the outhouse with Mom close by his side, holding him steady, we didn't see Paw leave the bedroom for three days. So, when he emerged in the doorway two days later, frail but standing on his own, holding a blanket tightly around his slender body, we were all aghast.

Michelle held her hand to her chest and cut her eyes toward the ceiling as if acknowledging that God was to be praised for his apparent recovery.

"What are you all looking at? I bet you hoped that would be the end of me." Using his rifle as one would a walking stick, he slowly lowered himself to a chair in front of the fire, propping the rifle against the log wall within easy reach.

CHAPTER TWENTY-TWO

Once again, we were all under house arrest, as Mrs. Derryhill called it. Although Paw was very weak, we feared him enough to follow his rules. His rifle was never far from his side, and Mom was afraid that in his current state of mind, he might do something rash. She explained to me and Roy Boy that when you don't feel well, you get cranky, and your crankiness can make you say and do things you might not normally do. She reminded me of the time I became too frisky, teasing Tippy, and he nipped my hand so hard that it bled. In my pain, I ran after Tippy and slapped his rump over and over until Mom called to me and told me to stop treating him like that. I cried, feeling sorry for the way I behaved and brushed the dog and sang to him the rest of the afternoon. I wondered if Paw would feel sorry for the way he's treated all of us after he feels better. I remembered the last devotion we had and how forgiveness is something God demands from us. I tried to hold no ill feeling toward Paw because I knew it was his sickness speaking, but whenever he barked his orders at us and mistreated Mom or Tippy, it was difficult not to think bad things about him . . . things I knew would not please God.

Paw managed to sip on a small amount of warm broth and a pinch of bread for breakfast. He slowly stood and wobbled his way over to the kitchen area.

"I might try to get some hot tea down my gullet," he said to Mom as she cleaned up the dishes. "Fix it for me, okay?"

"Show me what kind will make you feel better," she replied. I wondered why Mom asked Paw what kind would make him feel better when she is the one who knows the uses for the herbs. "I know you have your favorites," she added.

Paw pointed. "Gimme some of that last one and the one next to it. And make sure you put plenty of sugar in it."

Mom walked to the canisters and filled the tea ball according to his wishes. She filled the metal teapot with water from our inside barrel of rainwater and placed it on the fire rack until it steamed. Paw remained in the kitchen, leaning against the work counter. His pants bagged on him, and his legs trembled as he waited for Mom to finish preparing his mug of tea. Mom took a deep breath and slowly opened the canister of the sugar and poison mixture.

"The sugar's just about gone," she said, dipping the spoon inside.

"But Mom! Paw! That sugar's got poison—"

"Quiet, Effie," Mom calmly said. She turned to Paw and told him what I disclosed about Timmy eating sugar and refilling the canister with poison. Paw didn't seem too concerned.

"That's child's talk," he said, taking the spoon out of Mom's hand. "I've had plenty of this sugar, and it tastes fine to me. Sounds like something he told you to keep from eating any so he could have all of it himself." He chuckled, scooped out three spoons full of the white granules and stirred until dissolved. He dipped a little of the tea from the mug and tasted it.

"See. Tastes just fine." Paw shook as he walked back to his chair. Mom caught up with him and took the mug from his shaky hand and assisted as he sat. We all watched as he sipped. He noticed and frowned. "Mind your own business, guys. I'm sure you have something better to do than watching a man drink tea."

Paw seemed fine after he finished the mug. He leaned back in his chair and rested his head on a pillow Mom put behind his shoulders. She carefully covered him with the blanket from the bed, tucking it in around his scrawny legs.

"Let me know if you need anything," she said, going back to the kitchen area to finish washing dishes.

I was gratified to see that Paw seemed to be feeling better and wondered if maybe Timmy had told me that story for the reason Paw suspected. There was always a possibility that Timmy had been wrong when he said he replaced the missing sugar with the bonehead poison.

Just before it got dark that day Timmy, Roy Boy and I went out to play in the sleet that started falling. The cabin had become incredibly cold lately, but after we finished playing, it felt warm for the first time in a while. Compared to the outside air, the cabin seemed toasty. Mr. Bantom and Mike had been chopping wood most of the afternoon, for which Mom was very grateful. She slipped them an extra piece of bread with dinner that night. The rest of us sipped our much-diluted broth, to which Mom had stirred an egg into, creating her version of egg drop soup.

I heard Mom say to Michelle that the broth was nearly gone. She had made a large batch from the vegetable scraps and some bones from the last squirrel Mr. Bantom shot. The outdoors, being so cold the past couple of weeks, became our refrigerator and kept our supplies fresh. We stored what we had left in several ammo boxes on the porch, hoping a hungry bear would not find them and bust them open.

Our one, lone chicken had nearly quit laying eggs for us. I heard Mom say that we may have to eat it soon because "Man cannot live on broth and bread alone". Poor Tippy. We had to let him roam free and catch whatever he could to eat. Paw didn't want to share anymore of our supplies with him. The dog's dried food had run out three weeks ago, and his ribs were beginning to show. Mom was afraid he'd get worms from eating raw, wild animals.

I was impressed when he came home carrying a dead 'possum in his mouth, but the ugly, bloated thing smelled so horrible I had to chase him out to the open area to eat it. I wanted to throw up watching him rip it apart. Mom told me to be careful letting him lick my face now that he was eating things like that. She didn't have to worry; the sight of him chewing on that animal cured me of any desire to get very close.

Sleet and freezing rain fell for the remainder of the day keeping us from foraging for anything green and edible that may be left in the woods. Mom studied her books for hours on end to see if there were trees or brush that might yield a morsel she could feed us during the winter. She told me we had prepared to stay at camp for three or four months, but we were ill-prepared for the dead of winter.

Later in the day, Mom made the decision to kill the last chicken, saying that she didn't think it would survive such a long span of sub-freezing temperatures another day, despite our efforts to keep it as warm as possible. I walked outside, braving the stinging cold, to tell it "good bye". I walked around the pen and peeked under the tarp and saw nothing. I noticed that one side of its pen had been knocked over, leaving an open area under the fencing from which it could've escaped. As I ran to the cabin to tell Mom, I spotted Tippy's tail sticking out from under the right side of our porch.

"Tippy!" I yelled, hoping he wasn't stuck on something. I yelled again and realized something under the porch had his full attention, so he continued to ignore me. I walked around and understood why . . . he was chewing on our chicken and had pulled it completely apart. All that remained was a feathered wing, the chicken's mangled head and a few assorted bones with skin and feathers clinging to them. I dragged Tippy out and roped him to the porch post, away from his prized catch. Sleet bounced off my coat as I paused a while to think of what to say to Mom. She's sure to pitch a fit. But, knowing that Mom would be going out to get that chicken later on, I had to tell her the truth.

"Mom?" I said, where no one else could hear me. "I have something to tell you."

The look on her face told me she was frightened. Maybe frightened that we'd all starve to death. Maybe frightened about telling the others. I wasn't sure, but I could tell she didn't know what to do. She planned on boiling that chicken and using the bones to make broth, and meat to provide us with a few more days of protein.

Mr. Bantom approached us to find out what was wrong. When Mom told him, I could tell he was livid.

"Where's that dog!" he shouted. I remained silent. I shook with fear. Although Tippy did a bad thing, I still loved him and didn't want him harmed.

Paw woke from his nap and asked what was going on. The words Mr. Bantom used to describe Tippy violated Paw's rules about cursing, but at this point, I suspect all the adults agreed with him and didn't blame him one bit for his angry outburst.

"Gimmee my gun," Paw said. His rifle was just out of his reach, so Mr. Bantom walked to where it stood propped against the wall.

I screamed. The sounds that came out of me were wild and non-human. I ran to the rifle and grabbed it just as Mr. Bantom reached for it. I kicked him and screamed so loudly, he stood stunned for a moment before yanking it from my hands.

Mom stepped in and negotiated on my behalf. She told me to calm down then stood in front of the cabin's front door to block his exit.

"There's no need to scare the kids. Tippy is starving just like the rest of us and did what dogs do when they're hungry. Now put that thing down and come to your senses."

"I don't mean to be disrespectful, but that dog of yours has been mooching off of us, so it's time for him to provide us with something we need," he said. His steely expression softened, and his voice calmed as he turned toward me.

"I know she loves that dog. I love dogs. Had 'em all

my life. But they're just dogs. There's a time when we have to put human needs before their needs. Sorry little girl, but we're starving, and he might provide us with, well, some nourishment. We ain't got any chicken anymore."

"We can't eat Tippy!" I screamed.

"We'll figure something out," Mom said to Mr. Bantom. "Give us an hour or two to figure out another way."

"Ma'am, you've kept us all alive this far. I suppose I need to give you time to figure out what we'll do for food. I owe it to you."

Paw sat and shook his head, rubbing his forehead and pushing his greasy hair back out of his face.

"You're getting soft on us, Bantom," he said weakly. Paw got up and walked into the bedroom and flopped onto the bed.

"Effie? Did Tippy leave any part of the chicken behind?" Mom asked.

"A few nasty-looking things. Some guts and a wing or something." Realizing that she decided to salvage whatever she could and come up with a solution, I ran out the door without even thinking about putting my coat back on. The sleet and freezing rain stung my chapped cheeks as I bent to look under the porch. I tried not to think about what I was touching as I pulled out a few red parts and the wing. My fingers were numb from the cold, for which I was grateful. If they were not, I don't think I could've touched the squishy, bloody parts with my bare hands. But, in order to save Tippy's life, it was the least I could do.

The look on Roy Boy's face was worth the grossness of my actions, as I handed the parts to Mom.

"Here. I found these," I said, as Mom held out a bowl to receive my offering.

"A heart, part of the liver, neck bones, a wing. Was there anything else out there? Any other bones?"

Roy Boy looked as if he would get sick. He and Timmy were giggling and pretending to poke their fingers down their throats.

"A lot of people eat those things," Mom said to them. "Haven't you ever heard of fried chicken livers?"

They continued laughing and exclaiming and repeating "gross" over and over and teased me for touching the things with my bare hands, saying I'd probably get some kind of disease.

"I'll go look under the porch again, Mom," I said. Mom handed me the bowl to take.

"Make sure you wash your hands really well when you come back in." Mom wrapped me in my coat and tied a scarf around my neck.

"Ooh! You've probably got guts under your fingernails!" Roy Boy called out to me as I headed out into the frigid weather. All I could find were a few assorted bones with a little flesh clinging to them scattered around the area between the chicken pen and the porch. A glaze of ice was forming over everything making it difficult to see what was on the ground.

Mom boiled the parts I found and made broth. She added some flour to thicken it into a creamy, gravy-like soup. She called it chicken stew, but to call it stew was a little bit of a stretch. Whatever it was, it tasted better than anything I'd had in the last couple of weeks. Mrs. Derryhill was tentative about eating it that night for dinner but declared that it was better than starving to death. She slid every tiny chunk aside and inspected it as if she were panning for flecks of gold. No one asked what the chunks were, and I was glad about that. Timmy had a worried look all through dinner and ate so slowly, the stew must've been ice cold by the time he finished his small bowl. I surmised that all the talk of blood and guts he and Roy Boy teased me with earlier in the day was coming back to haunt him.

Tippy sat next to the table and begged for something to eat. When no one looked, I dropped a small chunk to the floor to quiet him. I didn't want anyone to remember Mr. Bantom's threat to shoot him and eat him and hoped that subject would never be brought up again.

Paw never came to dinner that night. He said he didn't feel well and wanted to rest. Mom asked him if he wanted her to bring him a little of the stew, but he turned down her offer. By the odor that wafted out of the bedroom when Mom came out, Paw must've gotten sick again. I overheard Mr. Derryhill tell his wife that it reminded him of the smell of death. She shushed him and said he mustn't let anyone hear, but it was too late for that. It angered me when she whispered back to him loudly, "We'd be better off if he died."

I entered the bedroom and had to quiet my anxiety by making sure Paw was still breathing. After the Derryhills' comments, I wondered if Paw would be okay. When I saw him lying on the bed, his eyes closed, mouth open and his face as pale as tonight's soup, I shivered. I'd never seen a dead person before but imagined a corpse would look just like Paw at that moment. I walked closer to the bed to see if he was still breathing just as Paw twitched and closed his mouth. Feeling comforted by this sign of life, I silently left the room and closed the door behind me.

CHAPTER TWENTY-THREE

Paw never came out of the bedroom the next morning. Mom slept, once again, in the living room with the rest of us, so she wouldn't disturb him, so she checked on him to see if she could bring him anything. I followed her into the room, but she told me to go back out with the others because she wanted to clean him up. Mom came out a few times to dip the wash rag into the pan of water she kept warm over the fire. Paw's room was so cold, I wished we could get him to come out and sit with us, but Mom said he was too weak to move right now. She hung a blanket on the back of a chair and pushed the chair close to the hearth to warm it. After it warmed, I watched Mom lovingly wrap the blanket around Paw as he lay shivering in the bed. He let out a soft sigh upon feeling it against his body.

Mom offered sips of water to him, but he refused. Over and over, she went out to the fire and carried back the warm, wet rag and placed it on Paw's forehead. Only his pasty face was uncovered. I stroked his face and asked him if he'd like for me to read to him. He didn't answer. Mom said it would be very sweet for me to keep him company if I could stand the odor in the room.

"Is he even awake?" I asked.

"I think so, Honey. Even if he's asleep, it might be comforting to read to him. Remember how I'd read to you until you fell asleep? You said it made you feel safe."

I had very few books at camp and didn't think my fairy tales would be particularly soothing since there was always a bad guy in them. I saw Mom's Bible on the table next to the bed and began reading to him from the book of John. There were many words I couldn't pronounce, so I skipped over them. Paw didn't seem to mind. He opened his eyes from time to time and looked at me. I felt as if he wanted to know I was by his side. I'd never known Paw to be afraid before, but I could swear I saw some fear in his eyes.

When Paw's breathing turned to snoring, I quietly left the room and set the Bible back on the bedside table. I blew him a kiss and returned to the warm room where Mom rested her feet on a stool. I repeated the thoughts Mom stated the other day, that Paw must've gotten into something he shouldn't have, and it made him sick. I looked at Timmy, who turned his glance away from me. I didn't want him to feel guilty. Like Mom said before, Paw was a grown man, and no one told him what to do and what not to do. So, if he'd gotten into something bad, he was warned. And besides, wasn't he feeling sick before Timmy put bonehead stuff into the sugar canister?

I asked Mom about the herbs Paw made tea out of, and she explained that some of them could have bad side effects on your body. She had not been aware that he'd been using them for tea, so that might be part of his illness.

I rested my head on the table, so Mom must've thought I'd fallen asleep, so she and Mr. Bantom spoke softly about Paw and his condition.

"It's almost as if he has a death wish," she whispered to him. "He's a smart man and knew that some of the herbs could be harmful to him. I think he must've been ingesting more of them than we knew because so much is missing. He never liked tea before, then all of a sudden, he was drinking it all the time."

"Right. Have you thought that there might be some reason why he doesn't want us to leave the camp?" Mr. Bantom asked.

"He really believes he's keeping us safe by keeping us here. That's all. What do you think? Do you think we'll be in trouble if we go back home?" Mom asked.

"Life will be different back home," he said. "But I think we should leave immediately, before anyone else gets sick from lack of food. I'm surprised no one has starved to death."

"We can't leave while he's so sick. There's no way he could make the trip on foot. And I won't leave him here to die. You can go back if you want, but I'm not going."

Mom and Mr. Bantom's voices were slowly rising, and others in the room were listening to their conversation.

"There's no way I'd leave you and the kids here to fend for yourselves. I don't think any of the rest of you really knows how to handle a firearm, and you'd never find your way back to town. The path is probably not clear anymore. I won't desert you all," Mr. Bantom said. "I'll stick it out as long as you do."

"I'm ready to leave," Mrs. Derryhill spoke up. "Just

point me in the direction, and I'll find my way back."

"You'd die from exposure in this weather," he stated.

"I'd rather die that way than from starvation." She looked at her husband, who pointed at the door.

"Suit yourself," Mr. Derryhill said. "I'm calling your bluff. You think it's cold in here, just wait until you start hiking through the freezing rain. And that creek will feel real good when you walk through it. Remember? We had to cross it to get here."

She remained quiet, wrapped her arms tightly around herself and groaned loudly, leaning back in the chair. Her eyes slowly closed in defeat.

Mike shifted the charred logs around on the fire, and we all watched as the unburnt ends burst into flames. Timmy took advantage of his mother's inattention and shoved some twigs under the logs, grinning widely as they caught fire. His mother had often told him not to ever go near the fire, but Mike, not knowing this rule, handed him small twigs to feed the flames.

Ever since the bedroom became Paw's infirmary, baby Josie stayed out in the living area with us. I realized that no one complained anymore about her crying or poopy diapers. The Derryhills and Mr. Bantom might be grown-ups, but it appeared they had matured just like us kids since being forced to live in tight quarters and unfavorable conditions. Mom was constantly telling us that we all needed to cooperate, act respectfully, and treat each other kindly.

Later that evening, Mom called me and Roy Boy to come to her in the bedroom. She told us that she felt Paw might be sicker than she had previously thought. I cried as

I clung to her, staring at the strained rising and falling of Paw's chest under the blanket. I noticed that his breathing, at times, grew shallow and rapid . . . almost like Tippy when he'd get overheated in the summer sun. He hadn't said a word to anyone all day, and his eyes stayed closed except for the time I was in the room reading to him earlier. I felt I knew what was happening but didn't want to ask Mom for fear of her answer.

"You, two, go on and try to get some sleep. I'll stay here with your Paw. I'll wake you if there's any change," Mom said. "Now scoot. Go join the others. I want some time alone with him. Okay?"

I rested in my sleeping bag on the floor in direct view of the bedroom door. Michelle sat up with Josie, rocking softly until the baby fell sound asleep. She rose and placed her in the padded box which had become her little bassinet near the warm fire, just far enough so no popping embers could possibly reach. Michelle bent down and kissed me on the forehead as I lay crying, soaking my pillow.

"Your Paw is in God's care, Sweetie. You're a brave, strong young lady, and I know you'll be okay. I'm proud of you, and so are your Paw and Mom. You're always such a big help to both of them."

She sat next to me, pushing my wet bangs away from my face. I grabbed her hand and held it close to me as I sobbed. Michelle leaned her head forward and closed her eyes. I watched her, wondering if she was praying or trying to fall asleep. Occasionally, she'd peek at the bedroom door. Her eyes shimmered wet with tears. Michelle and Mom had become very close during our time at the camp, and I heard her once tell Mom she thought of her as a second mother since her own was living far away on the west coast.

At some time, in the middle of the night, Mom came to me and Roy Boy and whispered, "I think you all need to come and see your Paw."

I gasped and felt my heart pound so hard I became dizzy when I stood. Roy Boy was stone-faced as he followed Mom into the room where Paw slept. I took a deep breath and stayed close behind him. While we stood next to Paw's bed, Mom went back out into the living area where everyone else, by this time, was awake and waited for a report.

"If anyone would like to come in and say anything to him, do it now."

Michelle and Mike took baby Josie into the room and said a quiet prayer and they stood next to me and Roy Boy. They left and made room for the others to come in. Mr. and Mrs. Derryhill seemed reluctant as they walked in with Timmy, who held his nose. Mrs. Derryhill gave Mom a large hug and shook her head as she looked down at Paw.

"Such a shame," she said. "He was so strong, now look at the poor man."

Mr. Bantom asked to have a moment with his good friend, and sometimes foe, so we stepped just outside the door, but not far enough so that we couldn't keep an eye on Paw. I heard Mr. Bantom tell Paw how much his friendship had always meant to him and that he'd make sure we were taken good care of. They all sounded like Paw was going to die, which terrified me. I silently prayed for God to spare Paw's life. Over and over,I begged God under my breath to restore his health to him.

I'd never seen Mr. Bantom cry until that night. He wept

like a baby as he exited the bedroom and headed out the front door of the cabin.

When Mom, Roy Boy and I, once again, had Paw to ourselves, I witnessed a miracle. Paw opened his eyes and smiled. At first, his voice was a whisper. We leaned close to hear what he was saying, but it seemed as if it were gibberish. As his voice raised, we realized he wasn't speaking to us but was carrying on a conversation with a figment of his imagination, behaving as an old person with delirium would.

"Nice to meet you," we caught him saying. He laughed weakly, coughed two times, and nodded his head.

"Mom? Who's Paw talking to?" I whispered.

She knelt down to me and said, "Honey, this happens to some people when their body is dying. My father saw his parents as if they were right in the room with him. It's God's way of comforting the dying, I suppose. Maybe they see loved ones welcoming them to heaven."

"But I don't want Paw to be anywhere but with us," I cried. Roy Boy whimpered, trying to hold in his emotions.

Just then, Paw said something I'll never forget.

"Knock, I'm so sorry. I didn't mean for this to happen. Forgive me. Please tell him I'm sorry and ask him to forgive me. Don't leave me, Knock. Please Knock. Stay with me," Paw said. He repeated this over several times until his voice was silent and his brown eyes closed. A peace fell over him. We held his swollen fingers until they grew cold, and his labored breathing ceased.

Mom kissed him on the forehead. Roy Boy and I did the same.

"I love you, Paw," Roy Boy and I said in unison. I

knew I'd never hear my Paw's voice again. He may have had his faults as of late, but for some reason, I felt only love in my heart for him.

Mom held our hands and took us back to where the rest of the group held vigil around the fire.

"He's gone," she said in a cracked voice.

"Let's say a prayer," Michelle suggested. Mr. Bantom came through the front door just as we bowed our heads. He joined our circle and held Roy Boy's hand as Mike said the nicest prayer I think I'd ever heard. He thanked God for Paw's life and asked God to forgive him and accept him into his perfect, beautiful eternal life. He prayed for me, Mom and Roy Boy, and asked God to take care of us, comfort us and provide all our needs. At the end of his prayer, Mr. Bantom cried out with a resounding "Amen!" and gathered me and my brother into his strong arms.

"You know your Paw loved you very, very much," he told us. We nodded our understanding and wiped our tears.

"Is Paw in heaven?" I asked.

"'Spose so," he answered. "He's singin' with the angels."

I couldn't imagine Paw doing that but was glad to know he was with God.

The men wrapped Paw's body with a blanket and carried it out the front door and up the path toward Mr. Bantom's cabin. Mom told us they would store it there until the ground thawed enough to dig a grave. The cold air would preserve him, and no bears or other wild animals would likely get ahold of him closed up behind the cabin doors.

Plans were made to bury him on the outskirts of camp,

just this side of the creek. Mr. Bantom offered to fashion a wooden crate large enough to accommodate Paw's body, but some convinced Mom that they would never be able to dig a hole large enough for a crate before the body started to decompose. Late in the afternoon, temperatures rose above freezing, so the digging of a grave began.

Mom assured me we would be heading back home to Burnt Willow very, very soon. It bothered me to think of leaving Paw up here after we went back home. I begged her to take Paw with us when we leave, so she told me she would send people back to get him and give him a proper burial in town once we got settled.

• ● •

The following day, the women and children gathered around the gaping hole as the men carried Paw's blanket-wrapped body across the barren garden toward where we stood. We stepped away as they lowered him into the hole. I bent low and set a photo and letter on top of the blanket, muddying my clothes as I hung over the side of his grave. I couldn't watch as they covered Paw with dirt. Only Mom remained at the graveside and stayed until the last shovelful was emptied. We had no flowers to lay on his grave, so we kids gathered any green foliage we could find and made a bouquet to place on top of the dirt mound. Michelle complimented us on our kind gesture and said she was sure Paw appreciated our lovely gift.

The last boxes were packed, and the men began

carrying loads of supplies down the path through to woods. For almost an entire day, we walked up and down the old logging trail, past the marrying tree and on toward the place where the creek had to be crossed. Mr. Bantom suggested that we leave anything that wasn't perishable or necessary locked up inside the cabin. He would plan a trip back in the spring to retrieve what we left. Tippy seemed elated to freely run up and down the path with us and stopped often to follow a scent trail.

"I guess this is the last of our supplies," Mr. Bantom said.

Michelle and baby Josie had stayed behind throughout the day but now joined us on the final trip downhill. I stood and perused the camp. I ran across the garden to Paw's grave and broke down crying at the thought of going back home without him. I looked toward the rushing creek and remembered my night in the woods after losing Bear Bear downstream. Bear Bear was safely packed in the first load taken from camp, and although the last couple of months were a challenge for us all, overall, I was sad about leaving Camp Marrying Tree. I thought about Mr. Chris and his disappearance. Maybe he was back in town wondering when we would return? I didn't like thinking of the threats made against him by Paw and Mr. Bantom, so I reassured myself that he'd made it out of the woods safely.

On our final hike past the marrying tree, I looked to see if my initials were still carved in its bark — a sealing of my love for Mr. Chris forever. I remembered my encounters with Knock at this tree.

One by one, we crossed the icy creek with Mr. Bantom's assistance. We took turns putting on Mom and

Paw's tall rubber boots, which Mr. Bantom would carry back over to the next person. Mom was amazed when the car started after only a few tries.

"I have a confession to make," Mr. Bantom said. He proceeded to tell us that Paw was correct when he accused him of returning to town. Paw, too, had left camp a few times to check on the garage in the middle of the night, so he wouldn't be seen.

He told us everything that day. All the ugly details of the business deal he'd made with Paw. Mom was angry. I'm not sure if it was because she felt Mr. Bantom took advantage of Paw or because Paw put his family in danger due to pride. Either way, time has now healed their friendship, and Mr. Bantom made good on his promise to watch over our family. He allowed Mom to keep the garage as long as Roy Boy and I were young. She hired good help and made the business more profitable than Paw ever did. Paw would've been proud, Mr. Bantom told her often.

Once I was grown, Mom cared no more about the garage and allowed Mr. Bantom to do as he pleased, in accordance with the deal he made with Paw. College is paid for, and my brother and I have good jobs to provide our worldly needs.

Mom never returned to Camp Marrying Tree that I know of. In fact, she never spoke much about it in my presence, and I did not pry her. Nor, to my knowledge, did she send anyone to retrieve Paw's body. I don't believe this was because she didn't care, but because she couldn't face the pain of bringing up memories of Paw's last months at camp. From what I heard around town, folks were told that Paw was mauled by a bear and dragged away into the woods, never to be seen by us again. I assumed Mr. Bantom had come up with this tale, and I didn't contradict it.

After my research was complete and my story written, I developed a desire to go back to the last place I saw my Paw. I miss him, and the weather is beautiful and beckoning me to return. At my brother's urging, I made my plans and mustered my courage.

Mr. Bantom is eighty years old now, but his memory is clear and vivid. Although he still owns the cabins and the land surrounding the camp, it's been two or three years since anyone has taken him up on his offer to use it for hunting. Mr. Bantom, knowing of my interest to go back to the site where we once lived, told me he hired someone a week prior to clear the path for easier passage. What a kind man! He rode with me to the spot where we parked our car before our ascent to Camp Marrying Tree many years ago. He gave me some pointers, went over the details of the trail and wished me well. I left him to nap in the car, assuring him I would not linger once I reached my destination.

LAST CHAPTER

The crude bridge over the rushing creek still remained – one Mr. Bantom constructed after we left Marrying Tree. I took a deep breath and continued climbing the hill toward the clearing where the camp once existed. With a bit of nostalgia mixed with notes of sadness, I looked to the left where the great marrying tree grew. Joined at the base, its branches now spread higher, wider and fuller than I remembered.

Memories flooded back to me. Knock. And the initials I carved proclaiming my love for my first childhood crush – Mr. Chris. Although briar bushes and vines had taken over the paths and places I used to forage, there seemed to be an area worn around the tree as if the brush had been crushed underfoot. I walked the perimeter of the tree's base, taking in every detail of it. I felt as if it were yesterday, the time when I expressed my sorrow and love to this tree. Knock's words of encouragement ran through my head and heart. I parted some vines, not poison ivy, but the name of this one has slipped my mind. There it was. I ran my hand along the tree's bark and felt the letters I had carved with the knife I swiped from Roy Boy in our childhood – "E.P. + C" was all I could read. *Had I written more?*

On the north side of the marrying tree, I saw something. Something I would carry with me the rest of my life. I stood on top of my "lookout rock" and stretched to reach the white object in the fork of the tree. The tack which held it in place fell to the ground and disappeared into the thick, forgotten-named vine. As I removed the photo, my seven-year-old face peered back at me with an innocence I owned "before it happened."

My Paw carried this photo with him in his wallet, proudly showing it anytime my name was mentioned. He was buried with that photo. I know this to be true. I put it in the grave after the men lowered him into that horrible hole but couldn't stay and watch them cover him with dirt. Had someone removed it after I ran away? I turned the photo over and my heart leapt within my chest. *"I love you, Lulu. Forgive me."* was written in my father's hand. I remembered how much I wanted to hear him say those words as he lay on the bed the day he passed. Under my father's message was written "Forgiven".

I did not recognize the penmanship but knew in my heart to whom it belonged. My intuition was always right. Knock was his guardian. Not mine. Of this, I am sure. I needn't seek anymore answers, nor did I have further desire to see the camp. I turned my eyes upward briefly, then began my descent from where the marrying tree stood.

END

Peggy Godson Mueller began her writing career while sitting in the carpool line at her daughter's school. Her car provided the quiet solitude she needed for putting her stories into written words. Fast forward many years. Her daughter is soon to be married, and Peggy's recent widowhood has shown her that life fies by too quickly. While life's plot twists temporarily took her away from actively pursuing her God-given love of writing, she is now back and eager to share her works through Winged Publications.

Peggy strives to create characters who are relatable, loveable, yet flawed. Building a little humor and sentimentality into her stories, no matter the situation, is important to her because real life is full of irony. Isn't it? Her goal is to touch readers' hearts and leave them wishing to know more.

Atlanta native, Peggy, now lives just north of the city with her daughter, Emily, and a naughty cat named Tinkerbell. When not writing, she works as her church's secretary, loves antiquing, and hanging out with family and friends . . . and, of course, providing a lap for her cat.

9 781959 788041